THE FIFTH SEASON

THE FIFTH SEASON

Stories By

George Angel

Normal

This book is the winner of the 1995 Charles H. and N. Mildred Nilon Excellence in Minority Fiction Award, sponsored by the University of Colorado and FC2

Published by FC2 with support given by the English Department Unit for Contemporary Literature of Illinois State University and the Illinois Arts Council

Address all inquiries to: FC2, Unit for Contemporary Literature, Campus Box 4241, Illinois State University, Normal, IL 61790-4241

The Fifth Season
George Angel

ISBN: Cloth, 1-57366-015-9
ISBN: Paper, 1-57366-016-7

Cover/Jacket design: Brian Pentecost
Book design: David Dean

Produced and printed in the United States of America

Some of the pieces in this book first appeared in the magazines *Caliban, Crescent Review, Eotu, Exile, The Iowa Review, New Orleans Review, The Quarterly, Quarterly West, Satchel, South Dakota Review*, and *Yefief*, and in the chapbooks *Globo* (Will Hal' Books, 1995) and *Las Meninas* (Picadilly Press, 1995).

The author wishes to thank Tim Fitzmaurice, Dart Lindsley, Michael Gendreau, Kevin Walsh, and Pete Davey, without whom this book could not have been written.

To Denise

Contents

Forgotten Story

From the kitchen window she may have been just more leaky architecture but the woman was a glass bowl from the beveled pane. The pale girl watches the whey faced myths gather about her house. Her box heart is a box of planed wood. She ran and run up to the high place when it was all over just ran and run your whole life to that place high feathered and slim shouldered where all the churches in the world anchored their bells. The wonder of it, a yellow tinged air like all the summers curtsying from their crannies. Tired children carry faces in their hands. The corners are sanded smooth where the joints slip tight. But what was it, more sheets billowing in the breeze and Sunday itself ringing the sunlight out of the morning, wringing a good wakefulness. My face washed and upright with marmish dignity even if my smile is a chipped plate or two. The trees are full of dead men. Her hands have passed over them so. That's all it was, ran and run all night through the moonlight with your skirt in your hands and yet in the high place what? Where was she going then, that day? Into the quiet water. Bringing back the empty bucket. It is night time and the house is a dialogue of grey and black. She has finished it with her most sounding words and her box heart holds what she has placed there, like a spice box full of lush dirt. The box light where her memory flickers returns little pieces of a backwards song that seem to float in wakefulness. A pomegranate, an afternoon, the chicken bones like twisted sticks. She sits alone in a room with a window. The dead rattle the change in their pockets. It is not nearly as breezy as you expected. The pale girl is dying by her window. The nature of a halo is at question here. The dead men are throwing their shoes at the myths but they continue to gather.

Go and fetch your dreams girl. The ball casement word held indented spoke its running lilysong hard.

Bring them back in a bucket. The mechanics of the high place is a socket. Work your day's length. A whirlwind running turned black and white by all the gears showing tight driven over and over under the surface of the moment. Meet the night hours with your pain. The pale girl's heart is a grey stone contoured like the first body. Turn it into something sweet bent hard when the sun comes up. The pale girl found a wedding dress buried in her garden. Return your ever widening wonder to the house you mend. The pale girl speaks skeletons of words already dead. Resign yourself to the small brass circle that is each day. The pale girl has a wealth of frayed instants. Mend the roof before winter. The pale girl grows thin has nothing but her shivering. Cherish the early evening. The pale girl sings couples into view. Watch the insects come in search of the fading light. The pale girl wears a yellow shawl in the evening. The pale girl had eyes that were too close together and seemed to buzz. The pale girl and transparent in the silence. Her dress lies folded on her bed. The voices of the pale girl become entangled. The pale girl is the arc of astonishment.

dim-bucket, house-word, tree-dark, oaths-in-the-feather, red-trees, sunday-clock, connected-weather, hand-halo, pocket-wakeful, skirt-breeze, night-frantic, gift-sounded, box-mended, hard-light, lilysong-shawl, myth-washed, kitchen-beveled, loom-hearted, song-plates, dialogue-broken, cold-forked, dropping-room, face-filled, grey-run, rib-windy, face-wheel, stone-wet, tinged-area, line-worry-resounding-box-of-children, box-of-maybe, ran-run, gathering-hard-songs, shard-flowers, curl-away-mended, from pale boxes they came gathering like small promises dressed as wishes to deceive the ringyear gnawing away at the roof and warmth of the house where, it had long been suspected, she continued to breathe.

From the kitchen window she may have been just more leaky architecture but the woman was a glass bowl from the beveled pane. The wonder of it, a yellow tinged air like all the summers curtsying from their crannies. My face washed and upright with marmish dignity even if my smile is a chipped plate or two. Where was she going then, that day? To see the children writing sea filled words? Naw, because look at these hands will you just I can't see my way through to anything remotely of a likeness to the rounded giving or the bold encheckered afternoon.

The pale girl watches the whey faced myths gather about her house. Tired children carry stone faces in their hands. The trees are full of dead men. It is night time and the house is a dialogue of grey and black. She sits alone in a room with a window. The dead men are throwing their shoes at the gathering myths. The area of the window is the only part of the house that is not run through with silver lines. The pale girl sits reading. Her face is quiet and the book is full of myths and dead men. Perhaps it is the voice of the child that makes her look up. You can smell the cold outside. But it is not nearly as breezy as you expected. The stillness gives what little light there is a resonance. The nature of a halo is at question here. The pale girl lives alone and childless in that house that was her mother's.

Her box heart is a box of planed wood. The corners are sanded smooth where the joints slip tight. Her hands have passed over it so. She has finished it with her most sounding words and her box heart holds what she has placed there, a spice box holding something the color of lush dirt. There in her well lit box heart sits a dull colored pomegranate, sporting its hips like a vase. There are the usual cut herbs and dried flowers. Holding it tightly beneath her throat, she admonishes her own gift with whispers. And though the box heart is dim with strangers, still visible are the grey winter socks and the sticks and stones worn bone colored.

She ran and runs up to the high place when it was all over just ran and run your whole life to that place high and feathered where all the churches in the world anchored their bells. But what was it, more sheets billowing in the wind and the Sunday itself wringing the sunlight out of the morning, ringing a good wakefulness. That's all it was, ran and run all night through the moonlight with your skirt in your hands and yet in the high place what. The box light where her memory flickers returns little pieces of a backwards song that seem to float in wakefulness. The dead rattle the change in their pockets. The pale girl sees that everything is connected. She ran and runs from her house in the dark, may her lover turn grey with oaths in her bed, she sees herself returning, not able to abandon her small child of three where it will surely die alone in her house, she runs and ran frantic from her sitting alone and dying in her house. The pale girl is the many beds of the stream where her mother tried to drown herself.

So and so and might have been if it had so but well I might have guessed the if and buts of it so yes and so please you and then the slipping down into the dropping room and yet you might have maybe'd but the and and and and of well remembered words if only through are a dark place where all the if colliding somethings found their namesakes and I tried to speak and I tried to write a letter but it became a fabric. Parts of the house collapse at night and then are whole by morning. I am always weeping in the main room. I am always tending to the garden. I am always finding a quiet moment here or there. I am always wondering what it is you are up to. I found a small place in my yard where I bury our child when I have gone insane. I am always waiting to become whole. I am always moving ever further toward—

The Dark

There are two children, in the darkness there. In the darkness, there are two children. Within the dim rustling, the sun has let loose fragments. See one pass the other without sparking in the shade. The silence leaves another fabric. The trunks of the trees rise, extensions of the shadowed dirt. Their green tops become dust-colored beneath the sun. The two children are moving there in the darkness like the sun's loose fragments. One child draws the other, simply by moving. The taller child is exhausted by the orchard. Lost within it, the smaller child digs stones out of the ground, filling his pockets. An area of light and their bodies become visible and then fragmented as they pass. The tight air holds one to the other, there beneath.

The soundless world has exhaled all its breath. The empty places are filled with some recalcitrant mystery; and yet the children move freely within it, denying it. The broadcloth of midday is plush with it. Perhaps this is the nest of memory. I see your face and then you move. For that instant that I see your face, the shadows accommodate its contours. How is it that these children are as still as stones beneath water.

As if gathered, the leaves lie grey in warm shadow, gathering the cold. There is ash on the small child's fingertips. Two dappled figures walk upon the solid earth. The ground is whole, and the passing minutes turn palm upward. The orchard holds the children. In and out of shapes of mosquitos and filtered light. The shadow is green. The silent rows of trees touch each other, there above.

The children's legs are brittle in the sea of dark, and the words they spoke earlier seem to linger like pockets of a sour smell. These words they have dug up out of their pockets with which they have covered the ground. They have passed these words between them, like bruises, since each first realized the other was there. The words

13

and speaker no longer mattering, just so that the movement in the words was there.

The children move and are lost to view behind the trunks of the trees. The orchard is empty. The trees hold the silence within the shadow. Small sounds are sealed to their origins by the dark. The orchard is full with dark. The trunks of the trees give off the last of the light. The two children come into view. The smaller child is somehow radiant. The taller child runs his hands over the trunks of the trees.

Alone, these children cannot help but be brothers and they are. Children are giants and they know it. My foot catches on something and the whole world falls with the impact. It lies tipped on its ear, waiting for me to grunt. The green world where it is dark. I leave the world tipped until it cannot hear the thud anymore. Then I lift the fallen pillar that is everything

The children move their giant arms and hold the world by a blade between their giant lips. Their slow movements are seen and heard by the small imaginary faces beneath them. All children can fly in the dark. The two children walk in their soft place. There is no direction, only filling the small spaces with familiar steps. Above the orchard, the sun is like a scribbled out word. Two children walk in the nestled darkness.

Like vessels, their faces float beneath the motionless branches. Perhaps the children are translucent, in the sunlight. Perhaps their faces ring upon the light like bells. This place is a bed of shadow. It is a stone in a dark pocket and the submerged part of a wheel. They stand within the still trees.

The children pass through the silence and first the seasons and then the years impose themselves on each other in the orchard.

Beggar

Beneath an oak tree. In the shadow of it, the cool of it, there he lay. Manuel, my poor Manuel. He had learned nothing in his life, and I loved him. The bees buzzed around his open mouth, so they told me. There, in the lazy afternoon, ended his days. What did they want from me, a cry for justice? No, you see, because I had learned.

The yellow sky drops its leaves upon the ground. Lying on the side of a hill getting drunk like a beggar, by myself, in peace. We are all of the ground and to have been something is to make a little jump. The afternoon is long and turning. None of them doubt my respectability. I have not been reduced to rags. I am alone with the snakes and birds. I tell you I am talking as fast as I can. What might you teach me now? His hand grasping I have seen already. Would you fill my mouth with blood? All rock retains the taste of skin. He told them and they have not learned either, when they put the ax into his head and I put his body into the ground with the echo of his voice: this is my land.

The breeze whistles dirty songs to my husband's corpse. The butterflies and moths mock the leaves. I shot the horse they gave him with his father's rifle because I did not know then that I didn't need to. The tall grass knows the language of fallen things. The old woman watches her legs dangle in the water.

If you want to know anything you need to dig into the ground. Pull the roots and see their fineness, how easily they snap. Babbling, and who would deny me this. I have become water. He went to them and showed them paper, and they turned into paper men and he was writing on them but they said nothing. He was getting to have a bit of a belly, middle age was kind to him. The garlands of falling — I can't seem to remember a single song to sing now. The twisted rope tastes bitter (he is almost here) and my tongue turns over. The house is away somewhere and all its windows and doors are open.

15

Mosquitos rest on the sheets hanging outside and nothing will dry because there is nothing in my sleep that I
might give to anyone. Learning not to sleep but to talk
over rooftops, the tall grass erasing with my talk as I
talk. Up above the trees, on this hill they have covered
with cow shit and the holes from their hooves, that
cracked the husband of a woman who did not know he was
only a porcelain doll.

I ask that you teach them slowly when it comes time
for them to learn why hair ribbons are tied in knots and
what happens when glass breaks, that they might always
remember it and always be learning it. Not my hand,
since I have learned, and his father's rifle is at the bottom
of a stream under the sand and flakes that are gold lies.
I am not as large as a tree nor as ruthless as a man. My
house is open and full of insects. They greet you with
clouds of trumpeting that will not be satisfied. I talk
when I would sing the silence of memory.

I am isolated by the silence of my chattering words.
This might give you some idea, loud and stupid and of no
use to the field, the one bird moving. The bead of sadness
has been pulled up out of me into the branches of the
spread tree. It lingers there, like moisture at morning
over flesh that is all pigs' flesh with its voice like a gold
ring, spending it on itself through its nose, where it
hangs. Gold light on water, gold leaf on water, gold boots
giving a dull sound against each other in the sand at the
bottom of bitterness.

It rains the impossibility of howling in a swirling
without direction I see in the impenetrable blue that
becomes smudged soon along the edges. If I had the
energy to bury this small bottle that it takes, drunken
and insane robins would swoop down and peck the heads
of those who would disturb me. I am within and he is
within me. It has taken me a long time and I have been
taught it without mercy, but I am within and even you
must someday come to me.

I am tired because I have been folding all the leaves,
and the moths are furious and night, hireling night, will

crush me and use the fine meal of me sprinkled in water to reflect the blind stars.

But please don't give me such a stupid face. You know quite well why I am talking to you. I am finished and blown off the branch with the yellowing year. Trampled beneath gold hooves. But I am holding this lost world, and you will have nothing of it. You are merely my errand boy. It rolls within me and sings. All your fires are spent on the swarm that crawls over you. My world will burn with an older fire. Its cinders will have wings to rise and then be gone. So your leaving means nothing. Remember. I send you out into the world, dead god, to prepare the way for my little child of straw.

Tres Tristes Magos

A=A amazes me. How anyone could separate a thing from itself, and then call anything by its name after that is beyond me. The world is a bouquet of seams, and without them even the first *A* is no longer needed. We are neither our shadows nor our pasts, and each moment's breeze is a birth as jarring and inevitable as the first. We are liquid in our casts. *A* and its *A* are spinning about its axis where *A* stands observing its two equal selves. Then there are three. Once the conception of the whole is lost, there can be no stopping.

We drift upon the grey sea where horizon is a myth. A hollow reed upon the rolling sheets of grey reflected light. Our imaginings have turned to gelatin. We were once perhaps a single voice but have lost the meaning of reunions. I have seen myself upon the street and ventured to make conversation, and yet when I approached, it was not me for my features were strange.

They were good friends. It was summer and the burnt white grass grew against the boards of *A*'s house. More of a large shack, it loomed dull and wooden in the blue. Out of the center of its roof jutted a squat planked spire. This was *A*'s workshop. The alphabet of tools glowed like arrows on the dark walls of the workshop. The air was wet and *A* sat at his work table as if a wire extended, taut and slippery, from his hips to his shoulder blades which were bare beneath his ruddy face. He understood sweat and the dust that finds its way into the corners of the idle hours. His overalls were faded with spots of something white all down the front. His work is filled with false starts, tugs, a fish in mid air pulling at the artistry of the drawn line. All men are dying. All deaths are speckled. The flash of each struggle curves and aches and rises. Beneath his dog eyes the stubble clings like a mood.

There was nothing for miles, and even then the road's gradual accommodation to the swell of the land could only barely be seen. *Jerry's* was a boarded little box beside the grey ribbon. An accumulation of shutters, a puny little pinch of hiding beneath the sun, this is what the outside said.

Inside *B* sat looking at his drink. The bones of his face cut at his pale skin, making it the surface of a chinese lantern. *B* sat waiting for the others. He turned on his bar stool to look at the small lit stage. He had sacred hands. It was small and only a foot off the ground. Its fringe was a thick green curtain, coarse, the color of sofas. A small round white space, as if something bare were showing through the surface of things.

C was the artificer in the garden, a crutch of green. He understood the flecked windowpane and helped it grow. There was dust upon the leaves of his life. He was short and fleshy and rude thumbed. He kept his days within his grasp with chicken wire and the spit of insects. *C* walked beneath the boughs of the cathedral, eating its fruit. It smelled like grapes and the stain of dirt. He knew the hiding places of form. The sun left a crescent on his bald head.

They were good friends. They met at *Jerry's* and drank, talking all the time of their obsessions. Daily occurrences, not the monumental, left their mark. Without point or direction, the anecdotes took their places like fish in a glimmering chain. One of them would mention something they had all experienced and each would talk about it animatedly. They put these things away and saved them.

There came a stretch of days that were empty, like a gathering of breath.

After the pause, a monument's weary impending fall sound of the hinge once again, they each dip their hands into the collaboration. It is a liquid that changes color and temperature.

First the feathered scramble over which moments it will be this time. The bag is opened and they come tumbling out. In quick succession, the spectacles of an old woman, attic light, a phone call from a forgotten love, hope, this house at night, your smile, a bell in an empty sky are all dismissed. For a while it seems as if they will make the smell of winter, which would be longer. In the end they decide to do two shorter moments: a yellow bush, the purple shawl.

Each returns to his workshop. He collects junk and scraps of things that catch his eye. More and more, sound finds its way into his head. He takes residence in the blind world of voices. He finds pieces of the sound he is looking for, but two questions plague him: are these shards of himself for him to claim? once whole, how will his own sound grow throughout the making? Slowly he begins to weld and affix and hollow out...

Each brings what he has insinuated to *Jerry's*. They practice making in the empty place. *B* has earned the right to sketch a skeleton for each object they are to create. When the voices of their insinuations first join in the air above their heads only structures are created. Subtly the sphere has learned a texture. Quietly it finds a ground and sends its stem. No one knows from where the yellow (so hard) glides down to rest lightly upon the bush.

B begins the next piece with a hushed caress. The purple stains *A*'s fingers with night. *C* widens what is made so far, making it intricate, making it lace.

The objects are constructed but do not exist. The three take their places on the stage for the birth of the objects. At times, two of them playing will balance out the third who is in the soul of the object. Or the making is playful and the object just seems like another one of the musicians within the moment. Two of the three will make more than the moment and rely on the third to remove just enough.

* * *

A Yellow Bush

1st movement
1. $B = \prod$ 2. $B = A + C$ 3. $\underline{A + 360°} = B + \frac{1}{2}A + 8\ (C)$
C (yellow)

2nd movement

1. $\underline{\text{C (yellow)}} = 360°$ 2. $C \neq A + B$ 3. yellow $(B + C) = A$
   $A + B$

3rd movement

1. $\dfrac{C}{A}$ = someone strolling by   2. $A = 9 (B + C)$

Coda

1. $\dfrac{\underline{\text{A (stillness)}}}{B + C} \cong$ afternoon

   2. $A + B$ = a patch of light upon the lawn
   C = the shape of it in the silence

The Purple Shawl

1st movement

1. B = the soft grey crossing bones   2. $\dfrac{\underline{\text{A + purple}}}{C} = B$ (caress)
   $A + C$ = her laughter

3. $\dfrac{\underline{\text{A (B)}}}{\text{her bare neck}} = \dfrac{\underline{\text{the purple seeps into her caress}}}{\text{the sound of crickets - C}}$

2nd movement

1. $C = \sqrt{\overline{\text{a single stitch}}}$ 2. $C + B - A = \underline{\text{a silver pin}}$
   holding her long black hair

3rd movement

1. $\dfrac{\underline{\text{shadow (purple)}}}{\text{moments}}$ = shaft of streetlight - B

Coda

1. $A^2 + B^2 = C^2$ 2. memory = $\angle\, ABC$

* * *

Spokes and spokes so grey, leaden splaying rays widening into the empty blue. A bright orange flag flapped from the back of the bike. The child's mouth was open and he bent his head just slightly to watch himself as he jumped the green bike off the curb and into the air for an instant before the decided tinny sound of landing and the tink-tink of pedaling off to friends and evening. Afternoon sun still put the world aslant. The sidewalks were orange with tilt and the parked cars seemed ready. Beside the house, a round bush turned yellow like the turning of a page, blooming with the fire of the descending moment.

* * *

Whose gloved hands have wrought this order? He who paced the hours and worried out the rose buds, tied the bloodied vine, mended each day's frost with words, nursed splendor from the aphids, tramped heavy-booted through Gethsemane long before its famous hour. We recognize the crumpled pants in the corner of the shed and we would have him back with us; for though he was anonymous and quiet, in his days he sheared the silence of its tentacles, and left us here behind the window asking merely for another moment.

* * *

Wires hung from the rafters of the high ceilinged place. Thin serpents down from the darkness ending in bulbs and microphones. About the place were vertical constructions, propped up or piled against the walls. An old fashioned machine spread its tenuous legs in the center of the floor. The two circular reels atop it were nearly spoked as we have seen. Figures sat sleeping in folding chairs behind the machine. Its base was littered with white styrofoam cups which lay overturned and drooling. Before the machine there was a street. A house upon a street corner, white with mustard yellow trim. Abandoned toys are scattered beneath the windows. This is perhaps a moment of rest, an inbetween time.

But the machine begins to move. It is on a track now. It passes before the house. It sees its reflection in the window. It takes in the sidewalk, the lawn, the hedges, the white boards of the house and a yellow bush. The track curves. The machine passes through the wall of the house and sees behind it. There is no inside to the house.

Wood beams support the facade. From this side, the wall is a membrane and intersecting beams have formed a web in the semi darkness.

* * *

Evening fell in particles of light. The streetlight shone upon her chest above the neckline. Her laughter was grainy. She walked along the street and she was laughing. Her long black hair seemed to be one sheen. Pulling the purple shawl up to her shoulders, she held her elbows tightly against the breeze. The passion in the throaty voice rises in an arabesque. The shawl is bright as fruit. You close your eyes and the light of it remains pressed against the inside of your eyelids. She is dark skinned and when she walks her heels click against each other. She is passing into the intersecting darkness, and particles of light are catching on her shawl and skirt. Dissolved within the distant web, she leaves you with a wealth of constellations forming. Your memories gather pinched about your face.

* * *

Rosa, we have shared each other's breath in the lantern light. The place is black and I go reaching for you. I create your spine with my fingertips. I hear you whispering to me. We have loved each other in the white house with the mustard yellow trim. In the silence, we gathered shadows for our sleep. I lie beside you and think of the Rosa I could see and hold and know. I remember our touch.

* * *

Late last night, two people were murdered in Hollings. A man and a woman, they are presumed to have been a couple. Reporters arriving at the scene found the bodies had already been taken away. All there was to photograph were the thick chalk lines upon the sidewalk describing the victims' silhouettes. The police would not disclose the cause of death. The scene of the crime was 345 Turner Drive, a small white house on the corner of two streets in a quiet suburban neighborhood. The identity of the two lovers has been withheld until their families can be notified.

The air has a sharpness to it. The news vans look slick and new in the dawn light. Well dressed people stand with microphones and point at the house behind them and tell us we are all in a hospital on the edge of town and dying of cancer. Flashbulbs turn the chalk lines silver.

The yard is plush with the morning wet. Joggers and neighbors in bathrobes stop briefly to look and then hurry on, disturbed and filled with news, to their respective doorways. A purple shawl lies entangled and abandoned on the trim grass. The police are cranky. The killer behind the hedge has struck again and not a coffee shop in sight.

* * *

Outside the making house, all is grey. The landscape is limitless, small hills like whales' backs extending past curiosity. The endless land is the only face that can be seen. The weary years have turned it grey. A voice might travel and find the sea which is but a softening of this, a corpse laid large and still in its mighty cavern. Whose voice is it that sounds outside the making house?

Ash implies a heat and once there was a living that ached as one and rose and fell. But its splinters have long since ceased their glowing. Once the conception of the whole is lost, there can be no stopping. All is grey.

Whose voice then?

Gabby

Gabby sits beneath the barn's darkness in its yellow warmth. In the straw with the smell of urine close and familiar. The straw like slashes all around him. Sitting sprawled in the straw and hearing bodies rustling underneath it. Feeling them rustling, warm like a murmur.

Luce, I got worms on my eyes. Can't see my own blackness. A preacher saying: Gabby you don't know any better but to look where your eyes are pointing, so they are pointing at the Lord now. Cause Luce I saw them and they think I am crazy cause I saw them and the worms are feeding on my eyes. Luce you are a soft-natured old gal, here with the warmth of your body. Cradle me in your softness, Luce. Don't matter about no lantern now, be finding you with my fingers. That's all right cause touch don't lie. You see the night but I know it soft, I know it cause I feel it on me, tickling me like one of your ears. Hush now. You been out today. All the way to town. I don't weigh much no more and anyhow I won't stand for complaining. Remember, you see the sun.

In the barn, Gabby rolls over on his face beneath the placid figure of the mule. He feels the wetness and the straw leaving slashes upon his face. He mumbles to himself and his body trembles in the chill.

You out in the sunshine. Doc, I says. Gabby I'm sorry, he says. What I got Doc? Cat tacks, he says. Is that bad? Those cat tacks will make you blind in a year. These cat tacks are the mark of redemption, I says. You too old for that, he says. Don't I know it, I says. And the sunshine of the last day as the worms get long and fat on my eyes. I can feel them scratching. In the straw like piles of slashes. Laugh and you begin to hear them rustling like they shamed. Bodies clutching each other, the slashes like whispers and snakes twining their arms and legs and I saw them.

The light is blue. Memories with wings crouch in the shadows and have not yet taken on the smell of cobwebs.

They tremble there, their wings membranous and quivering in the black hidden places. The yellow light is gone. Its blue sheen lingers upon Gabby's face. As man and mule move, their outlines are a little slow to correct themselves and the black shapes elongate, becoming other shapes. The song in the blue light is a gentle song. Its archways fill with starlight as the outlines touch. *My fingers don't lie to me. Your flanks have burned them the color of ash. The streaks of dirt are there running back from my fingernails. As if they were leaking.*

My fingers are fleshy and age worn. Their blessing is upon you. Luce, your gentleness ain't like a woman's but like a child's. See here, soft like sleep. His luminous face just above the line of the mule. *Here I am, Luce, yes here. My eyes are quiet but my touch can whisper.*

Birds and crickets can be heard through a hole in the barn's roof. Sounds sliding down the shaft of moonlight which strong and almost solid cuts the barn in half. Man and mule beneath it, as wonderous as pilgrims, thankful for protection from the cool vastness just beyond the barrier of light. Outside the trees lisp quietly night's unending continuation.

And what is in Gabby's voice? *Luce*, he says. Like a red liquid in a clear tube. The muffled sound sheathed within the throat as if the throat itself is merely more snakeskin unfurling and dissolving as the sound lingers. His arms over the stretch of mule. His arms like the spokes of a blue wheel in the grass. His hands pass over the mule, soothing it. Following the grain of the mule side. The cold reconciles man and mule. Gabby presses his cheek against her side. *You and me, Luce, we are going to get out of here.*

Outside, on the roof of the barn, his memories speak among themselves beneath their wings: Where were we? Did we know of him? Could we see him there where he lay in the barn under the mass of mule in the yard of our very heritage? Yes. Memory is not a caged thing, nor arthritic. We are the sum and the light. Our voice has lit the hanged man and the underside of a leaf. It continues to sound as if to censure possibility. *Might have been* and *is* and *was* is all one word. Our voice, our eye, is without limit or agenda.

The little orphan girl Clara that the *Patrón* had adopted because she was his niece. From the beginning she had the look of one. Her skinny chicken legs dirty where she squatted in the mud. She looked up at Gabby and he thought: Naw, too early to tell.

What's it like being old? her eyes laughing up through her bangs.

It's sad, he said making a face and then leaving her because then she was fifteen now and her chicken legs had changed and she came up behind the barn and showed him, an old black man, something. *Clara you quit that* but his eyes were watching and his thoughts said *child you fetch yourself to the water, it will clean you; you ain't got no choice but to drown yourself now, you don't know where you're going but I know it.* Gabby turned his face away and the girl laughed and ran.

I know it, Gabby said to Luz in the silent barn. *Cat tacks for the Cat Man. Luce, me and you got no place here. Us and the moon will hang heavy and pass over the night. No blade is going to cut that mist. Rest up Luce and we'll wait till just about too late and then no breeze around here is going to hear our names for sure.* Gabby was thinking to himself, no longer even looking at the mule. Instead, he looked at a woman who was not there.

I know it, Gabby said, *but I ain't got no money.*

Gimme them shoes then.

These shoes here? Gabby said. *What do you want these shoes for?* Gabby waited. *These is the only shoes I got.*

Them shoes is all you gonna get too. Gabby tugged them off sullenly.

Come on over here Honeyballs. Quit making that face cause mama's gonna make it all feel good.

Gabby feeling her press him to her. Gabby has honeyballs as he rises and falls upon her. Knowing the smell and sweat of her as he looks into her outraged face.

He makes a sound down deep in his throat each time he moves upon her. She clutches as if he were about to go somewhere. Gabby looks up and sees his and her silhouette on the planks of the shack's wall; the two bodies merging into one large animal heaving itself, vomiting. (Walking home barefoot. *Señor, I ain't got no zapatos. Como? I reckon they just perdido.*) The two bodies stop and start again. She says, *You ain't paid for this,* between clenched teeth. They pass from lust into a numb country and their sweat dilutes the pain somehow. Nothing left but the very rhythm of it. She saying, *Soon as you stop I'm gonna cut them off.* Gabby's eyes pulse with the pain of the movement and he peels off of her; watching her catch mouthfuls of breath, her body still, as if she's hurt.

You and me Luce, we are going someplace where they ain't never heard of sin. Seems like we ain't put here for nothing except hurt. In the stillness a barn is a chapel. Lost souls and sounds are just more huff of wishes in the breeze. Night, every voice an explorer in its mansions, has claimed the whispered altar and the shambly old man before it. Gabby and the mule standing in the straw.

The barn was blind with cricket light. Phosphor as fast prints on the ceiling's ribs, as nettles in the skin of his eyes, beneath the roof hovering: enclosed. The soft light had given in and been pitched upward, rising, slipping with its belly like a seal on the angle of ascent, and smack, right through the roof's timbers and out into the evening air that already grieved its innocence.

Each placed on the night like a pinch of life, houses clustered here and there all along the rise, each the glimmering feeling of voices held between your cupped palms. Houses, and who first dressed the heart as a mechanism within a room? Gabby was a sheen unfolding like the wings of something oiled and black. His trembling lips mumbling all around the mule like a brown ribbon unwinding wild and almost silent but for the sound of the mumbling of a brown ribbon. Pull in the net whose strands in the shadow leave slashes on your face and coddle the huddling nerve.

Gabby smoothes out the mule as if he were ready to lead her out of the barn and then says *Naw*, and lying down, *we'll wait till just about too late, ain't no use hurrying.* In the barn Gabby rolls over on his face beneath the placid figure of the mule. The wet straw leaves slashes upon his face. His eyelids slip down over his eyes and his vision is made perfect. His body is encased in a black cylinder where orange flashes fill the emptiness. The feeling is friendly and internal. Somewhere in his mind the thought passes that this is what it will be like when he is completely blind. He feels the cylinder begin to move and he knows that he is not quite asleep and that the blackness is just sleep coming on. The old man nestles his body into the straw.

It is a bright place in front of the *Patrón's* house. Gabby is down on his knees and the wind is brisk. His sight is flashing on and off, one second he is out in front of the house and it is very bright and the next he is slipping off to sleep in the barn again. There is a dog running about him where he is on his knees. Gabby feels the heaviness of his own limbs. The dog is tan-colored and just full grown, very playful. Gabby smells straw and feels its itch. The dog is rubbing against Gabby's side. He pets it and it whimpers happily. Gabby mumbles to himself and his body trembles in the chill. The dog jumps up and puts its forepaws on Gabby's shoulders and begins to lick his face. It is unimaginable that there is anything outside the barn's stillness. Gabby tries to push the dog away and he can't. The dog's claws are cutting his shoulders. We are at the hole in the roof of the barn and we see Gabby on the straw in a nest of light. The dog begins to dig its haunches into the front of Gabby's hips. The dust from our wings turns the moonlight the color of chalk. The pressure of the dog's haunches is painful and Gabby pushes at him but nothing happens. The dog continues to lick his face happily. We have returned to him now, we were all of him anyhow.

Worms get off my eyes! That dog ain't through yet. You are getting ahead of yourselves. Cat tacks quit your cutting. It ain't my fault I saw it. All right Lord, say it is. Say maybe I had what you might call a talent for sin my whole life. What then? It ain't but a sickness. Why are you going to take away the colors in the world for that? The seeing was like a fever.

She had come to live with the *Patrón* ever since his brother, her old *patrón*, was killed. Her name was Aurora and she was a deaf mute. She brought Luz with her as her only possesion. She cleans the house and fixes his meals.

Summertime and the heat of it on Gabby's face. Chasing the damn animals in the yard. The grass already having that burned look to it. Chasing one of the animals, Gabby looks in as he passes the window.

The *Patrón's* room. Their clothes on the floor. The white of the wall turning their bodies brown. The rocking of their bodies as they entwine. Whispers and snakes passing over their skin. Her hair where it has stuck upon her cheek. The *Patrón* as if he is praying within her. Their clutch like a flash. She is on top of him and passing her hands over the *Patrón's* chest. Their bodies are like arms of light. His lips passing over her slim belly. Everything else in the room so dead, so immovable. Watching their bodies get louder, like something rushing forth to kill itself. And there was something in their hearts. You could tell by how they held each other. The way their hands were sure they held the other's body and yet not giving up on the moment, still frantic. The bodies quit moving but the lips continued and there was something quiet in the caress and after. Gabby shooed a fly from his face and realized he was trembling there at the window. It wasn't sin but tenderness that blinded the old man.

The old man in the barn felt the little dip of slipping from consciousness and then into a thicker place where nothing moved, not even himself until self became lost and there was a rumor of a sensation so vague that it was mere wishing that kept existence going. On some sort of hum inside like a high wire with no chance of falling, simply continuing on the thinness of it. Gabby began to dissipate.

His body became lighter on the straw. At first it was just a rustling and the sound of the straw exhaling. Slowly Gabby's body rose beside the mule until it floated about three or four feet off the ground. It hovered there, where the shaft of moonlight caught him at the chest. The straw beneath the body still held its indentation. The mule nuzzled up to Gabby's face now that it was up at the height of its own shoulder. There was no one in the world but Gabby and Luz in that barn.

One by one, each of Gabby's memories climbed (their wings had long been unserviceable) down from where they waited in the hole of the barn's roof. Each kissed Gabby's lips lightly and then without any sound of goodbye, passed through the black rectangle of the barn's doorway and out into night.

Not even the mule they found, standing alone and harmless the next morning, knew what happened to Gabby after that.

Evolution of a Blue Line

The blue word shines upon the insect's ink, the edifice of rhythm. Night is a white shade that will not be honeyed by lamplight. Night is a white drift behind the unsounded skyline and the word is a shadow in the drift.

Half the hour is a moment filled with snow that is not there and whose absence leaves the smell of oranges where oranges have never been, and the other half is an afternoon of bones piled like firelogs every twenty feet in a pasture of tall grass, welded grains and mumblings, imagine.

Were it not for a fence of milk and wire, this would be the neighborhood of the word. In the distance the word is mistaken for a mountain but is only a bottle on a fencepost gathering the image of the pasture. The chicken scratch on the edifice shimmers, a bar of colored light behind the white shade, it has a family of wishes to lift.

The blue man wears his gestures like falling water. His heart is in a bottle on someone's desk. But he himself is liquid, in repose within his sound. A jacklight in a sky that is all clouds. His hands are stained upon his lap, making vertices in the world of oranges. The blue man breaks and falls, unhinged in tributaries under cold breezes. The moment smells of fishes and whispering old men while the blue man sits broken waiting for his tree.

But what about the land about the land about the color?

The land about the land was a wrinkled sheet that sloped gently down into the indentation where the body had been. The brown lines formed the silhouette of the light. Then they became translucent, superimposing upon each other, ridges and trails that were the rain's face. Slipping upon sediment down, down on the murky ground to the rounded pasture whose voluptuous bulks were green, whose rocks were like uncracked beetles.

And the houses?

And the houses, that small and white and hunched

between thick trees, as if they wished to merge with the hills and basins, stood behind their painted toy fences and seemed ready to forgive with their very forms.

And this is the home of the blue line that may have been a word and may have been a man?

Yes, this was the home of the blue sound we heard. Because it bent its spokes and caged itself within us. We spent our days divining its containers. It left its sad rumor on hard surfaces. The blue sound was grey, when we found it in a tarnished thurible abandoned on the cobbles of our own dream like the bloody and beleaguered visage of the Baptist himself, having remained too long in the company of insubstantial things, such as our dissipating hands and smoke.

And the fabric of our hands was and then but if what you call the then is so you might when the jitter of a but between the only quicker with your soft meantime of a prayer you so you do if perhaps a but the well you needn't can a will of huh you say but in its heart my please it can't your face where if it waits a second if but please we well remember and that it can hold my if you will my heart outside our remember and but yes well but and you my if I hold so we that if it were a remember I might needn't between quicker us than jitter at our meantime if that please a prayer of a well but second outside I know remember and jitter meantime hearts of my can and will be gotten through our if a prayer may so receive our huh respected perhaps my well quicker perhaps of if it were like a glass box that had so many needn'ts that our ifs were cleft by gotten over warmed prayers and there you have it if you will but look outside remember a prayer if trapped within a glass receives a meantime or a heart between our please but yes and but you we if yes I knew our how had yes even if it hadn't quicker meantime so remember.

But the chapel, well, a fine thing. Full of bells and intonations. Just passing over the threshold fills your mouth with lye and oranges. Though the wood rises in arches like the innards of a guitar, the inside of the chapel is light itself. The hard surfaces here, graven images of their own putrid suspirations, are gone about their weekday business while the marriage of voice and light stands up proper, underpinned by two sticks whose revels have ended in a marriage of their own.

There is a flying thing in a dark place walking along the ground. Does it walk in and out of a cone of light, or is the light blue and diffused? The flying thing picks its way through the silence, keeping its head low, studying the ground. The flying thing has a battered appearance, disheveled, as if it were recently beaten or tortured. Traces of fear linger on its face.

With its slow deliberate walk, the flying thing traces patterns over the empty ground. It is attempting to fill the space with its walking. It feels the pressure of de-rangement and yet its movements are gentle. It is fright-ened by its own gestures and so contents itself with walking. The dark place is becoming increasingly vast.

The flying thing comes to a wall. The wall seems to be only a few feet tall and wide. This other presence somehow comforts the flying thing. It cautiously cocks its head at the wall. It is curious as to the texture. Its frail head bobbing jerkily, its eyes trace the mortared lines of the wall's surface. Left and up and in two and over shaking to nothing. Strong up and right and up until branching into unimaginable. Veins in the sturdy squawk-ing that carry empty places to the deepest part of thick. Grey and a flat coarse touch, the landscape of this dark place is a plain with its river of stone.

See the flying thing and the tree of mortar in the wall behind it. Because the flying thing has turned its back to the wall and stands still, watching. It is made of tangled wires held together by pieces of clay and cloth. It is spindly rather than gossamer, comic than graceful. Only the nervous eyes are solid. The rest is scrap and spit. There is a spot of dried blood on its neck.

Cloth and Clay: It all depends on a length of rusty pipe between us. It does. Yes. What. It. Yes. Plumbing is a main concern at our age. What. Our age. Yes, mystifying.

This grey building and the lengthening watermark on the ceiling. Our grey age. Yellow is a comfort on our tea cups. What. On our walls. Yes. On our fingertips and teeth. Our sad age. Blood yellow by now. Yes, perhaps. Not an ahem in sight. Well. The thing is not to appear to be looking for one. The movement of it though, might go unnoticed. Yes. Well perhaps we ought to go out and get a bit of air and see if we don't spot one. My rheumatism. Yes. Perhaps. Perhaps. Might do it good. Yes. Well. Well. Yes.

The sun wraps an accordion around its circle but cannot tempt blue to stain the sheet it rests upon. Blue is dead in an unfinished coffin his relatives stand around, shivering shadows from their feathers. Blue's hands are thick and you would think they would have stuffed him in a bottle with fingers sticking out like a bouquet of unwashed creases. But they have not, and his suit is hazy around the edges.

Cloth and Clay carry the casket out of the mourning hover. The excitations and small children crouch in sideroad ditches, watching. They are silent as the procession passes, trailing all its minimockers behind it.

Home

Yes, the boat was too small. The fishing was good however and Joe had been a regular on these trips for about four years when it happened. We never thought he would go over the side, his body suddenly in the water as if it had been snatched.

* * *

It is very windy beneath the structure. The cold is like sleep. There is a hum.

You walk between the buildings of corrugated iron. You can't make up your mind exactly what the trash that fills the street consists of. There are spray-painted words and shapes in bright colors upon the buildings. These look like wounds. You don't look to the end of the street because you are lost and you will not recognize anything here.

From between two of the buildings a dog comes trotting out. It is old and mangy but is moving at a steady pace as if on the way to some place or business. Its eyes are completely white. It is moving at an angle, its hips seemingly offset from the shoulders by age. Anticipating its course, you see it is moving toward you. You try to get out of the way but it compensates and heads straight for you again. Its mouth is open. It is missing large patches of fur where the pink skin shows through. It seems unconcerned with you. There is a sound deep in its throat that sounds half-hearted rather than menacing. It approaches your leg. It cowers and whimpers as you go to kick it. Then rather than a lunge it gives a sort of quick duck and you feel its teeth in your calf. The pain is dull and it is rather the animal's physical proximity that panics you. You begin to shake your leg wildly, and with your eyes shut you hear the whimpering commence again between the clenched jaws.

You look. As you shake your leg, the dog seems to

come apart with the movement. First you see where the skin splits and begins to tear. Then you see the eyes roll out of the sockets. In your violent revulsion you accidentally step upon one of the eyes. It is as hard as a marble. The muscles and appendages are falling away now. You watch the dog's entrails slip out between the ribs. You can hear the brain in the dog's skull, as wet and soft as a sponge.

The dog comes completely apart. At last the purposeless jaws fall away and clack upon the street, still snapping open and shut for a moment in their own remains.

You feel the cold passing into your blood through the holes left by the dog's teeth.

* * *

You feel weak. You are sitting with your back to the corrugated iron. You smell its rust. For the first time you notice it is night. An old man approaches you from across the street. He is carrying a blanket. He is your father.

* * *

Who is this old man, eh? And a blanket, my friend. How many times must I tell you then that love and man are the same word. Your scorn amuses me. See the patterns in the blanket upon your very body. You act as if I were a forgotten phrase. See there, the phrase is repeated. Who is mad then, eh? Warm yourself and remember that you don't need a heaven to simply love this, feel the passing of this.

You and your heart are a duet, my friend. It speaks to you and you to it as if you were separate and unknown to each other. This to me is sadness. When the song can no longer find its singer I weep for them both.

Bend your head closer then and listen to a story much like your own. It is the story of my son Joseph and his wife Margaret. They too are separate from their hearts. They are a quartet parting at twilight. They are old in spirit and the story is not about them but about the dialogue of their hearts. His only friend is his pipe, when he can find it. Her only friend is the indian summer in which she can dissipate, where everything is fuzzy with beads of sweat hanging like notes. The mandolin, you know?

There was some horrible accident. He is blinded by it, my son Joseph, and does not know it. He believes Margaret is a ghost, that she has died in the accident. Or she has died, I don't know, and from where she stands she does not know that she is only a ghost. She thinks, where she stands beyond petty time and pulsing life, that he has been blinded and cannot see the her which does not exist.

In any case they are without each other, without starting point, you know? Do you remember yet the things which you have not experienced, you know, like me, confused? Well this language their hearts speak is like that. The mandolin again, then. Yes, of course their hearts still talk; I said quartet didn't I? It is a strange tongue that passes between their hearts:

She says to him, "...And I went down there too, don't think I didn't. The sea was lead, a blanket of grey shingles. I could feel my silhouette blurring, my very sense a quivering. I was there as we had agreed. The sea was silent and along its stone corridors I searched, but where were you?"

He to her, "She sat upon the terrace, a curved response in its glare. The bowl of figs in syrup upon her lap, holding each mouthful before her eyes, heavy and wet, as if it were a question."

You think you hear the old son of a bitch laughing as he tells you the speech of their hearts, but I am not laughing. Sadness rings in my ears, single notes louder and then softer changing tone. Ah, as I said, confused. I point to my head and you laugh, right? Keep yourself warm in that blanket and listen.

She says to him, "Joe, over the years I've forgotten what it was you wanted from me."

That ringing in my ear a trumpet or french horn or both, playing just the single note.

He to her, "And my desire for her would seep up through the cracks in the floor beneath the bed, like melted wax, translucent and warm."

This all a dance of their hearts' voices, she says, "What good are walls of bone? To recline within each socket, worn smooth with passage?"

And him, heavy with wishes. "Like a tongue, wet and interior. If only shadows were what it passed through then it would light each shadow like a figure in a room, slipping through the centers of those days that propped up against each other were like panes of glass."

And now yes laughter. The last recourse of sorrow, right? Because here they sit before the television, on the couch, old, and he is blind and she is a ghost. Their hearts facing each other and they facing the television having forgotten how to weep.

"Margaret? Margaret!" he says upon the couch.

"I'm right here Joe."

She narrates the television program and he is frightened because she has become so much harder to find since the accident. She places a sweater upon his shoulders so that he won't catch a chill.

Even in his blindness his heart sees something: Bold black lines within his eyelids, straight and random. These lines form small areas of color between, green and grey and the color of flesh. Then these bold blacks lines move and combine, becoming luminescent until what he sees upon the dead surface of his eyes is a wood beam frame of a house, naked and glowing in the blackness.

Within him the voice (confused right?) resumes the dialogue. "An embrace is not the bloom, merely the entwining stems. The bloom is just above the lovers' heads, somewhere beyond them."

And she at last attempts to retrace the steps, "Just the scent of it unfurling as if from the weathervane's beak. I smell it Joe. How could you have ever thought that a gesture, of all things, would cuckold you."

Here his heart is silent; my sad son.

But you don't believe all this about hearts talking. Just listening to the old rooster because it is cold tonight and you have nowhere else to go. Confused, eh? He has given you a blanket and now you are smiling and lonely. Old bastard, right? Goodnight friend. May your memories be kind to you. Love and man the same word. Remember. Adios, eh?

* * *

Suppose it is a table or a house. Let us say a house for now, an enclosure. There are no doors or windows, merely dark spaces of entrance which make the walls between their cool toothless mouths seem like the legs of a table. It straddles the afternoon breeze. Its walls are smooth and white. Grey wisps play over them, shadows of a deeper purity. See there behind one's noticing the clumps of dying colorless grass.

Its blended coloring is that of a dream, a place where someone dead or forgotten is met in those moments just before waking. Place it in a desert but it is not there. Speak of its structure and there is nothing but a murmur, no wood or mixture to speak of. It is squat beneath an instant's lucid sky. An instant in which tender jagged notes are heard adorning a simple word. Because there are figures joining hands upon the structure. The area between these figures is as blue as backdrop. They are pink and faceless, inhuman with hope.

Eyes closed, one draws yellow lines through the night air outside this house. Geometric webs trembling as the notes pass through each strand untouched. One's head aches and the heart is empty sailing closer just above the enclosure, never inside. The brilliant rectangles of light within, hung on the walls like paintings, are a memory. The notes descend like a bannister embedded with scrollwork.

This must have been in his head, this house, when he stopped thrashing about and sunk beneath the water.

We straining our eyes and shouting. But all we saw, and this only for a moment, was the tip of his hair brushing the surface of the water like an eyelash.

Western

The further palm, the feathered spires hang red with faces. He hung around for awhile. There were several small words. Bob, whip, bull. They stood like stick figures over the blue and pink. Small insects inlaid as our fingers passed over them. The hard-edged wandering words. A blue net that felt like a stone wall, like the dried wax there. A blue net filled with small stick-figured insects. It was beginning to chip and the blue flakes were pink on the other side as the breeze caught them and hurled them back into place as the clouds drew back and the day drew back. He used to sweep up in the back there. His words are small and hard.

Checkered, the whole coffee shop unfolded in red and white checkers. The sounds came around the bend, came out around the corners, emerging from avoiding out around the mass of voices that were clean and sharp as geometric shapes. I heard his dark shirt over the chair finding its place in her room where once her hands had shaped the rain into a chipped dish. He ate his eggs. The window filled with hillside, making the shape he cut out of it dull-colored and downward. A hard-edged field at sunrise is covered with tiny blue bottles. Yellow has a way of avoiding the furrows, making the ground like a sponge covered with house paint behind the side door of the garage in the shadow with the web perhaps feeding it, with its touch or with its milk. The sound of his lips as he chewed his food said he and the woman were married but they were not.

You will always find playing cards in the trailer and bottle caps on the floor of the filling station. So see with your hands. Find the cold around the cup of coffee and the sweat in your hat. Peel back the leaves over the ground and the moisture that seeps up into the cloth over your knees. What will you find? Noon with its nervous children throwing stones?

Dip the evenings in wax and see how the curvature

of the spine dome sky rises flesh yellow calcified. Beneath it all the little apron romances, with the house behind them hardly three dimensions, acted out as if there were moonlight and sorrow and a bird. Heave high your gazes that you may lift yourselves up by them. This the bald head and the man of cloth that never was there before them. You gathered up your faces on the surface of the headlights and waited for the flesh to resound as solid as the light but only glass on cotton place mats in a dusty room.

Their faces were sheer. Their eyes were pylons with curbs underneath. Their mouths were words cut from sheets of green metal. Their cheeks were warm. And they sang sad songs. He stood with one knee beneath a guitar everyellowing.

The two, it is assumed, will die. Slipping absolutely around their uplifted hands, slipping from where they stand. In a place, perhaps two, where this and that and those meet like the thin metal rods in the center of the umbrella. Under hands red from soap, the clean sky pressed, unfurled, behind us. Their faces soft where they sang and harder elsewhere.

The mechanic collects their bones in a wheelbarrow. He has always been a collector, when she loved him, when her bracelets sounded behind his ears, then. He is all zipped up. There was something going on here. Picking up everything in this little tin there. That's how it works. A voice. Every moment is a mechanism. A yellow box with small flowers painted on it with a thin brush, with care, with her face in mind, or perhaps the blue oval on his chest which says *Tom*, or *Bob*, which are not his names.

He was the mechanic, they superimposed like that. Maybe it was their intents, that's all, finished. He parodies dusting his hands against each other. It is a very cold day, or room. One of the two. In any case, it was a good day. One of the two had loved the other one— curtains, smell, hard, memory, touch, sound, the deeper color in the wood, reddish almost, a voice, the dirty pane itself—all through it now. What would be the worry now

if —yes a big hillside where everything gathers and the
upended songs lying about. He was the mechanic. Not to
say that she was not mechanical. He and the mechanic
would fight quite often, you see, and she would be left to
her own devices.

Red words, red words. Sounds everywhere and him
supporting himself by painting red words on flat pieces of
wood, just to tell the passerby this or that.

Huddling, swirling up like paper junk up around her
heels and up, her face. Only birds wear feathers, but
complicated and light like that. Like the bones in a big
tower.

Oh yes, they'll be dead soon.

Making all the fluff and powder for the birds huh.
Big chunks of it if you dig deep enough, the earth itself
coagulating as it closes in on its heart. Big reddish wet in
your hand leaving your imprint hard. Of what then? Had
he been in the service?

There was a cap somewhere, god knows, and maybe
faces in the windows of the garages as he came up the
street. Again the essential words. Singing in there somewhere when the sound turned just so. Rising to it and
touching.

Assured then lost again.

He kept his tools in a rustling box. It was a dark box,
and light caught them where the grease had not. It was
a clean day when he kissed her and the metal that was
always before him—changing colors.

Up and to it. Up and her hands upon the window. Up
and at it. Perhaps the service. Perhaps pretending there
was a soft shape or form or sound.

Ed was a hard word. Ed sat in his blue Buick. His
hair combed back so that the grey looked like down on his
hard nut. The downfalls, sour as yellow paper, clicked
behind the creases. His mouth found its nest in his jowls
as he mouthed away pieces. I am tired. You don't know.
You speak and the sounds have the implications but you
don't know. I could hand you my glasses. Thick with dust.
I could say smell here, and indicate. The sweat would

pass into your skull but you would make it young and a flecked mirror would press against your features and the sky behind you. I am small, and my wail like my shoulders hides inside my bulk. The seat is wet against my back and I say please and stand and still no breath and land and, and still no breath because there never was the possibility of stepping out and into something out and into something that had not been there before so that it and I could evolve at once or one of us choose not to but no. Always one of us is finished before the meeting ever takes place.

Ed runs his bony hand over his hard nut. Oh you know, yes. I used to have something like that that it reminds me of but I can't place it directly in my mouth. I used to wear a bit in my mouth and I can feel the bone in my jaw compensating for it now. I fancy I might take myself a fall. Leave the damn wheel for a quick tumble in the dirt, barely a scuffle, a meager puff in the dust, and that would be it. The sound of the keys left in, expanding the land everafter. Ed places his face upon his hands and his sparse bristle is reminiscent of something.

Then some rest.

The wind sounds once, and the tension on the surfaces is comforting, a rhythm. He and the mechanic are playing cards in the front room while she lies dead on the bed reading a magazine. The rug curls up there, a hole in the screen door here. The sign painter is disgusted and the mechanic's mouth hangs open. He watches them both, folds, lets them play. He listens to her voice humming something in the other room.

Yes it is four o'clock. Yes the wallpaper is yellow. Yes the mud is on our shoes, dried, worked, clinging where we have stopped breathing. But this is all very small change. The dog is dead and we smell like folks. Yes the radio. Yes each of us will fall dead in this room, or not far from here. When I die you won't be able to hear it anywhere. Like dying in a jar. And still we press each other's fabrics to our faces and inhale because we find each other's softness there. So that she might sing. So

45

that she might laugh, so. So that the jets might sometimes leave chalk marks on the sky.

The bed is all a world. The blue sea is hiding black-
ened shapes. The sail is high and flat. Everywhere the
little boat would go the sky is filled with words and the
people are smiling. Their teeth the sail their teeth the
pale ovals all facing out toward flip the bed toward flip
her face toward what do you want toward tired flip yes
the world is an open space.

The kettle lies a few feet from the faucet in the
yellow grass. And then I sleep and the dead weight of
pictures on the pages slips sulking down the bedspread's
curve I know it close. Sunlight and breeze heavy sleep
almost. The earth is reddish around here and hangs
together the deeper you go. Worry down, down to the
deepest sound. There is an orchid inside my head, in the
dark just like momma had.

The sad man caught in the fence. He bends and pulls
and still no sense or use away from his limbs caught and
bundled in the wire. His hat on the ground behind him.
His green pants how they are held, his green shirt. A
shadow leaves only the anguished oval of his face. Its
features the isthmus of his stack of heaving. The breeze
has lulled his heart to rest.

His head is a grey stone. There are nicks and
scratches on its surface as it tilts. He pulls and cannot
pull away. The stone seems to rise and then it rests. His
veins and the wire are entwined. His blood is the orange
color. His mouth speaks from the grain in the posts,
leaning slightly forward, its cry held solid in the wood.
The man pulls and then is done.

He rests and is silent. He pulls and cries out. The
small stars have found his arms and legs. The sad man is
carried by some specific sensation. Within his rising cry,
his face there, within the thick hair upon the wire. The
grass around him is wet and green where he cannot fall.
The place is quiet where he hangs green. Making up the
bed of rivers and moving water, large grey stones worn
smooth beneath the water where something had attempted

to catch and grow, but could not.

It is hot here and the air won't move, like enamel, like one of those fans on the ceiling in the movies. Like his sad face in the doorway, like wishing, like wanting to take a bath, like he puts his hand on my face and repeats something, something for me and I put my hand on his face and still the air won't move so I ask him something and his face becomes tinged and is beautiful but there is nothing to breathe and dust settles on everything so I press my face to his and something changes but nothing moves and the world hides in the magazine.

Then she stood up from the red and white checkered blanket where they had been lying on the grass. He watched her there, a few steps away, beneath the yellow sky. She turned toward him and he smiled as if he were behind the wheel and they were driving and it were the convertible. The old primer-grey convertible that had been red before memory got tired. He would have pulled the tarp off that was always over it and jumped in as if it were all youth and speed. And she would think *where to*, as she was now, as her momma who had died violently and young had thought. This fear of her own restlessness reassuring her now that this was all very distinct and the hillside and sky and man were all changing and vivid and she was not dead as long as the air got cold at night and made sounds that frightened her.

I am not at home. This is what she would have said to the desolation of just wanting and finding nothing but more passing flesh. He smiled again and she wondered at their disconnectedness. Which one of them was really the cur. Her face paled and she tried to smile too. She walked toward him and kneeled down on the blanket once again. He turned over on his stomach and looked away up the hillside. They were passing an emptiness back and forth between them. He smelled something sour in the ground. He was sick with quiet afternoons and waiting.

Place - light - chill - slope - faces - up - moment - hung - sweater - October - key chain - dusk handed - return - one eye half closed - sky upon the land - damp -

sharp - well lit - blanket - sun - recall - silver bracelets - voices - mother in the car - crickets - entwining - sermon - sound - path wound - the dim shadow of the house - grey shapes in the breeze - the back of an arm - shadow - drop - remember - bottle - fan - sleeves - snoring - window - ice box - smallish - smoke - cloth cap - vision - names - bathed - mean eyed - place - television light - cupped - slipping away - trash smoke - eyes above the blanket - word - held - ceiling - bolo - matchbook under a leg of the table - nylons - hack saw - eye shadow - the battered bicycle - brushes - a wicker basket with green plastic flowers on the front - can I - bucket bucket - cast - mother lost before the light is gone - cast - mother - mother reel in - sound - reel in.

There is a car in the middle of the field. From sometime in the forties it has come curved and smooth and humming. But it is no longer humming here in the middle of the night. Its front has been smashed in and the tires have been removed where the pale grass brushes the wheel wells. The body of the car is light blue in the moon's light where the rust has not made it darker. The head lights of the car are somehow on. She passes before the two beams of light and attention is initiated to her movement.

Following her movement. Her head the dust lifted by the breeze into small turning shapes and all for mute. She cannot speak. The place she is moving toward is a lie. The words she has brought up are lost with her. Her body holds her past like a cup, like cupped hands. The man without movement. The man imbedded in resin. The remorse at their having touched. The small grave in the field that holds what. *The child*—these words are lost with her. She walks on into the dark and still from her come all the words around her but not of her. She can no longer speak. Her words have been robbed from her where they lie upon the little stone. So many hands and not a world to touch. She can no longer speak. All the magazines in the world are fluttering as silent as water.

She walks along the bed of the creek that has dried

up like her words. It has left striations on the season's mud. She knows she can walk between the silent banks for miles. The trees on either side of her bend toward her. The crickets are remote and the air is sad here. Then she passes into nothing. She walks along the strings of a guitar. She can no longer speak. She has been unstrung.

She walks between the hands of the creek. The air was warm and dead. Perhaps there was a house or store or highway, some source of light in the distance, too far away, and so woven into the fabric of the darkness. Indistinguishable, except as a pale spot where the thread had worn bare. She walked on and the sky and dry mud seemed to be converging toward something. Her feet came down softly, without direction, honoring only the idea of a general movement into. This is what it is to be lost, when time no longer has any agenda for you. She walked between the banks of the creek at night.

She is suddenly conscious of what her hands are doing. They were there at her sides. She brought them to the back of her neck but she was not tired. Her skin had the feeling of suffocation and then a vague lifting with the rare breeze. The air of desolation was strangely tropical.

She disappears into the darkness. The faint light gave up its touch. She is lost to view but for a portion of arm which dimly lingers. She is gone. Does she die. Does she weep beside her child's grave. Has she gone mad. Has she drowned in nothing happening. Is she a drunken woman. Does she return into light at some later time. Have her disappointments made a bed for her and the unmoving man. Is there a magazine near her hand. She disappears into the darkness. Is she a corpse wrapped in a red and white checkered cloth. She disappears into the darkness. Is she young. She is gone.

She can no longer speak. The sound has hunched its shoulders. It is in her throat, an animal without breath. She bares her teeth in the stillness and feels her chest rise and fall. She has made herself over as a basket for the sound that will not lift from her. She is not dead or dreaming, this is a common night with its common walk. She can no longer speak. Has it been a gradual process, her words building nests within her. No, for they are sinuous, muscles extending the length of her that can bring forth no movement. How long since supper and the edge of kitchen light. The movement out away and in the darkness is irrevocable. She can no longer speak. Is even the urge lost. Do you need light to speak. No, because the whispers and the murmurs and the touching and the apologies that would rather have been tears but were too tired.

Silence is a territory she has found. She and the man in resin could now touch if they could move or speak. She traces the line of her jaw with her fingertips as his would. Has she continued walking. She can no longer speak. Is there a tenderness like a trophy in this.

There is a stone inside her. Inside of being lost. As if it were a fist, then smooth, passive and immobile in its center. Curled inside her dark and cradled. She holds what she is engulfed in, lost. Hollowed out, a wooden figurine. The stone moves like the tongue of a bell that is sealed off. All of her lost except for the stone that huddles there. She can no longer speak, unseen and hollow. The empty movement, with hands outstretched, reaching for what. Grasping at lullabies, she hums something to her cradled stone. Her hardened self rolls about within her.

She has a stone inside her. Like a small head nudging in the belly. But immobile, rolling of its own dead weight. With her arms she caresses it and nurtures a hidden heart. Smooth and hard and clay, it wears grooves within her. It is something she has found inside herself, when she slips unfurled and silent into what.

Perhaps she continues walking. Or sees the light of the house. Or rests on a bank of the dried creek. Perhaps there is no more walking and just the small hard sound.

Hand - song - weather - slope - down - flew - out - doorframe - her hair - shadow - wound - sang - sang - sang - bullheaded - jar - red - white - red white - fixed - sourgrass - crow's feet - handle bar - salt - arm over the back of the chair - recollect - spit - dance - resound - fingernail - laughing - cactus in the window - clutch - sunup - carburator - slippers - candy apple - radio - window speck - handles - worry - place mat - knick knack glass knick knack china - shrug - face against the cool glass - button - creased - wait - flies behind the house - wait - thimble - wait - tinge - coffee - wait - wet - wait - channels - cup - stations - light - buckle - smell - stain - welt - murmur - light - standing against it - rough weight - hallow - spare - rough can on a string - sad - silent - washline - breeze's caress on an empty dress - splinter - beetle - a small face laughing - brown bottles in a paper bag - steps - dog on a chain and the tin bowl - sink-rack-stack- of wood - shelf paper - cards - moustache - our bodies on the bed in the still air - world - song - hand - arc - down - last - wait - word - wait - last - down - wait - down - under - wait - ground - weight - slip - sound - down - weight - stop roll - sound - roll.

This is the way things fit, the way they come apart. There is a scale. Things are placed on it, things are taken off. Objects are falling. They are losing their grip on whatever they are resting. They fall and land and slip off again and fall and land and slip off again. The sound of their landing is like a great percussion.

Things are packages. They make smooth passage. Outside the house, a strand of barbed wire wraps itself around the head of a dream. The dream stumbles. It continues its wandering over the expanse. Its hands are extended out before it.

Outside the house, through the halo there, the sky is propped sour with hillside. Passing through the strait halo like a window separating voice and landscape. Passing through the singer, everything, sky hillside expanse breath, seems to be propped forward and flat. To lie upon the plane of everything in hopes of some within.

Outside the house, along the highway, there were wood signs everywhere dark with shadow. The words on them were like a rattle. It was this but that might those. Best if you best so come best my best. Coming up the only life for fifty miles so stop, huddle up, mumble your grumbling pennies and move on to more life and more coming up your clean air. Well, then, this your that my yes I well you might. Yes.

Outside the house, along the highway, a bunch of old boards hang in the shape of a house, curiously suspended. They hang there as if on strings, all sign of paint and glass gone. The wind blows trash and spiders through it. The smell of a sad child passes over the expanse and fills its spaces.

They saw her mother before they even saw the car. Her body was there in a bundle on the pavement. Her lips seemed to be pouting, her hair drawn back neatly from her face. Her eyes were shut and the eye shadow made her look like a kid. When they reached the car the radio was still on. Her mother had told her strange stories. About a woman who had left her husband up in Michigan and taken all his shoes with her so he couldn't come after her.

Outside the house, silhouettes make cracks in the morning. Figures hundreds of them, with flowers in their hands, cover the expanse. Their faces have the feel of a brown bag.

The sky is yellow. The glare comes off the dust. It is the main street and all the windows are painted with names and gold leaf. The street is dust. There are walkways made of wooden planks. One of the windows holds the painted word *Saloon*. Before this window, two or three horses are tied, and their flanks shine in the sun. A player piano jangles on for a few seconds and then is silent. The wind lifts the dust in swirls.

There is a woman's face in a window. It is expectant, tense. It is visible just above the dull line of the hitching post. She is wearing some sort of bonnet. She looks to the large clock and its white face is blank as the hands slowly come together, as the bells begin to sound. The hands have come together against her will. She is a spectator of her life. She presses her face against the window. Everything will come undone without her moving a finger, without a sound where she waits behind the window.

The glare on the street is blinding. The wind comes up again and the swinging doors of the saloon flap emptily. The street is deserted. Usually there are wagons and people, but they are all hiding somewhere.

There is a light jingling sound. It sounds again. It comes from two small metal stars that are attached to a pair of leather boots moving along the wooden planks. The sound of the boots coming down on the wood can now be heard.

As if in echo, another pair of darker colored boots, with the same spurs, moves along the opposite walkway. The two pairs of boots are approaching each other.

In the saloon, a small man wearing a bowler and a watch chain gulps down a shot of liquor. And a woman with a large bright feather in her hair yawns loudly as if she were bored or sleepy.

In the silence of the main street, two men step off opposite walkways and walk slowly to the middle of the street. They face each other. They are dressed similarly, except that one has slightly lighter colored clothing. They are both wearing guns whose handles are clearly visible and whose hammers glint in the sunlight. The leather of the holster softly pats their legs as they walk toward each other, slowly.

They squint their eyes. One has a look of hate, the other of determination. Each raises his elbows away from his body. They have stopped walking toward each other. The face in the window looks sad more than anything, almost self-absorbed.

The man with hate in his eyes says, "Draw."

Shots sound out and one of the bodies crumples and - and - and -

And laughter. Yes, of course. But within every stylization there is a gesture. And the small book with the bright cover did not assert bravery or romance. At least not to the eyes that passed over it. Because these eyes had long ago given up both. No, these eyes passed over it for the same reason they watched the lightning at night sometimes. To these eyes the small book asserted that there was something at stake. That within the silence there was something lethal that you had to be aware of. Because if you weren't, maybe they would find you somewhere. Someday they would come upon you where maybe you had been lying for weeks and there wasn't much left.

Within every shape there is a stone. Within every bird there is a stone. Within every tree there is a stone. The sky with its large brigt stone. Within every woman and man there is a stone. Within every kiss there is a stone. Within every memory there is a stone. Within every promise there is a stone. Within every shape there is a stone, calling it back down into the ground.

manque

I cartwheeled out of the throat of the thing, like a caricature bending up into a cloud hovering beneath the roofbeams. The fabric of it was slick and when it caught the light shone back peach-colored. Lace-framed and flushed I walked into the orange woodlight. So then a spire rises like pressed palms and in the clinging hook and line of touch fronds serrate the empty clouds. The lawn is a continent in the gardener's palm.

I cut the pew-stained air, a pendulum naked as cherries. Oh I am coy, but what of this. The empty dress walks onward. What do I want from these moments, oh I suppose, and yet am I to expect this poverty of ribbons? Bent upward in the air away from a tide of fingers. A miracle of fleshes passing up through the voices like smoke that turns the very thought of skinsongs grey.

And then a him? Please, must I contemplate a him? No, as I said, I slip up through the frill collar and out into the air where only the Sacrament and I dwell in brittle silence. Bless these spindly limbs and let their naked grey shadows hold hard the drab and greensour piety of paraffin and crossed sticks. Nailed upon the heavy smell of owlwives, sweaty legs and sooty petticoats curling like bent wires in his mouth.

God bless the dust in the shaft of light, for in it curls a young girl's eyelashes. Wear this thing! I won't, I say. As if the Virgin were a clown. As if the throat of a bird were merely a finger for a ring. As if things forked and grew in the ditches of the aisle.

I am curled up I tell you, away, lifted. The censer turns my bare breasts the color of ash. The empty dress walks on toward what? All this merely the fabric passing over my face.

But there is no seam in my imaginings. My head pops out through the collar and into the light and the rest remains strapped in place. Your faces dimple and giggle. They press together, cheek to cheek, like the sides of a coal chute. I slip on them down to this silly idea of a him.

Focal

I. Four Tall Poles Standing

It was a matchbox on a piece of paper, its curtains were white and see-through and made a fuzzy sound when you rubbed the folds together between your fingers. The outside was high and white. Its front and sides were rectangular and flat, its windows all identical and regularly placed. Its two storeys were only discernible by the second row of windows. The door could not be imagined to open, the way it was flush with the front wall in the center at the bottom, like a rectangular mousehole. It must have been constructed just before the second world war by someone who believed in monuments. There were no shrubs or vegetation of any kind besides the pale green grass that stretched the entire property and three or four solitary trees in the back. There was a small guest house and a tool shed toward the rear of the acre. The house and the garage were separate buildings with separate strips of concrete leading parallel out to the street. It was on the corner and its land was four times the size of its neighbors' making it seem alone, shut off, above; the light shining brilliantly off the white walls.

But you care about none of this because you remember the musty smell of the carpets, your Grandmother's voice, the huge stairway rising from the center of the lower floor, the upstairs rooms that made the neighborhood seem like a map, the toolshed with its dirt and rust and its dusty closeness, the guest house filled with boxes hastily moved as your Grandmother made small talk in her soft pale voice, her fingertips resting gingerly upon her collarbone in surprise, and the joy in knowing that you could not run from one edge of the yard to the other without running out of breath as well in those windy hours before dinnertime of that last spring.

You were visiting, and visiting was a temporary thing even if it was just a few blocks difference. It was like being pasted onto the wall of a room in a doll house. Tables and beds were foreign and the world smelled funny. There was age everywhere, and this quiet was the strangest thing of all; you were left alone to the mystery of your own territory.

The brightness of the ice cream truck was blue. Its battered roundness was the color of eye shadow. A blue lion sleepy on the asphalt. The notes rose off it like flies. Something about the music just seemed to curl and rise, gilding the walls of the house with fossils and striations in the shape of figures running. Patting them into the smooth surface with hands that drip muddy water.

The world is no longer windy with Sundays. You can't hold life within a sweater and it had gone. Now we are always in this territory of Thursdays. The eternal touch of light upon the doorstep just before dinner. Perhaps Grandmother is too feeble and has no one to fix it for her. You needn't worry. She has passed on, dead I mean to say, and now the outside is moldy with ladders. Men wearing little masks move over the walls like twine.

The land itself was an expanse. It seemed to run away from the house at the back. Its flatness a synonym for distance. Children passed over it like a huge rake. The house had some sort of agreement with the sun. Rather say kinship, and leave at that the soft glare, like a breeze almost, that resolved the house and made the grass pale. In the brightness your outlines got fuzzy. You were lost somewhere toward the edges of the expanse, playing at being lost. Drinking in the fever of the hot days, twirling in circles like a disc on a string until you fell and the sky spun away from you as if you were sinking, lost and sick. Complicating the air around you with characters you stepped out of every time you moved. Giggling because their bodies littered the grass and you didn't have to pick them up because your Grandmother couldn't see them. Tired because you had to carry the weight of all their talk inside with you.

A tide of shadows around the house. Washing up higher, the dark planes blacken before passing into the house and out of view, only to reappear on the other side high and dark and then long and thin blending into afternoon. At night the house is submerged in shadows that are only held off by a series of roman arches which extend from the walls like spider's legs, forming cool corridors along its perimeter. In the orange light of morning the arches are withdrawn into the smooth surface and the house is once again a high sullen cube on the cloth of grass.

But they have turned the house a pink powdery color. Men who walk over the grass with the familiarity of conquerors. The guest house resists like a puritan as the bulldozer assaults it and finally knocks it off kilter, wrenching it free. They have parcelled off the land and two other houses soon rise against the sky, emptying the back of light. They have ripped the skyline from you. In your mind all that is left of the old white and solitary house are four tall poles standing dark as matchsticks beneath the clouds.

The men are hanging nails upon the mist. Imagine that, a sheet unraveling and rippling crisp on the wind. Bundles of money tied with fresh ribbons of concrete like the walkway that cuts up the center of the lawn. New blood informs the stream of seasons. For a moment the fat lady looms indecisive on the sidewalk, like a fleshy smudge of life in the cool air. She has a native starchiness that is endearing. Her hair and sunglasses give her an unbending aspect, while the hem of her light green dress is a bit high for the times and hints at a netherland of pulpy white thigh. She is not a creature of the outdoors. This breeziness is far too much for her. She retreats to the known comforts; the door of her burgundy colored car shuts with a tidy click. The windows are immaculate and tinted green; and while a passerby might remark that from outside the car the fat lady looks pickled, from inside the world has the look of an undersea kingdom. The trembling bulldozer almost looks amphibian and the red and white bow of her own trailered boat protrudes dependently from the foliage.

Let's go at this whole thing once again: There is something in the land, say two or three feet above or beneath its surface, that is place. You walk about it each day as if it were there. You find in it the history of your encasement, in the end all you have left. Of this land is this house. It is a small ornate jewelry box, inlaid with pearl, which will not open under the pressure of your hands. The fat lady is a coin within it, catching the light, like some foreign currency that cannot guarantee your passage.

Again: The house cuts out a place for itself and its doorways are the mouths of the current. The tributaries are finding each other and merging, gathering force. A current of land as place as passing as the smell of sweat and supper as the screen door rattles with the youth of your returning. An altar of seasons engulfed by the current. A current toppling schooldays with transformed playthings now webbed and sticky. The doorways empty onto the streets where the sculptured grey has met a deluge of tendernesses and lost its coherence forever.

The first time you saw the big burgundy car it reminded you of assassinations. The agent drove up in his own. He approached the burgundy car on foot and spoke good-naturedly through the lowered window on the driver's side. The day was the color of cotton. The door opened and the greying man in sweatshirt and jeans stepped out. The two entered the house and once the front door closed behind them you were irrevocably outside.

Now the burgundy car just makes you think of the butch boy. He sits alone upon the grass. Sometimes he rides his skateboard up and back on the sidewalk in front of the house for hours, as if to catch the rhythm of it. When anything passes, the butch boy pretends to flip his skateboard at it and then gets an enormous charge out of this.

It had heft and forward looming, this house. The quality of light could be cool. There were greens and blues in its moist white winter. It wore an ambuscade of witnesses like a coat, a coat of crickets and wishes. The angles in a gem form buildings, and in this way each stone is a skyline. The butch boy goes looking for his winter but all he finds is the austere vineyard within him. He stands like a spectator in the field of crucifixes.

Nostalgia is a sour smell on the air. The men turn the place pinkish with their guns. Their machinery curls with rust and whiskers. Their guns make that hushing sound. At night, the milky plastic they have hung over the windows filters the light. Seven or eight people sitting in the front room with glasses, their features stained and runny through the plastic. Off to one side the white piano braces itself against the tinfoil colored wallpaper. These faces are pinched yet loose skinned. Their grey pallor hints at some remote greatness and somehow justifies the alcoholic banter. The sound of ice cubes makes these people want to embrace. The men are bulging and romantic and tired. The women are somehow geometrical!y solid and are staking out their territories in the room, wondering whether they or their thin haired counterparts are the actual victims. For a moment you see them as stuffed into their clothes, as oblong packages wrapped in brown paper and tied with twine moving on a conveyor belt to the little wet bar and back. The night breeze plays with the nerves between your shoulder blades. You press closer to the window light. It never occurred to you that someone would wear a bow tie in a private residence. Are cocktails really the color of gasoline? Or is this just a notion you have from seeing these people's expressions as they swallow? The negotiations in the front room have lost their joviality to the heaviness of alcohol and the hour, and the starched couples begin to eye each other and silently plan their escape. Outside you are disgusted by their stumble and clutch. You walk over to where the gun is resting on the driveway. Pulling the hose behind you, you begin to paint in the pink powdery color, sealing the windows and the door. It takes a great while but you are getting a feel for it. You decide to paint the lawn pinkish as well. Pacing the property in neat rows, the job is eventually finished. The effect is immensely satisfying. You paint the fence pinkish. You paint the sidewalk pinkish. You paint their cat pinkish. The burgundy car looks good pinkish. It is much more than you expected. Everywhere you look, objects are blushing. The sky even takes on the tinge of laxative. You wait for them by the door calmly. The night is young. The shadows evaporate in the door light. As they come separately and in couples you blast them. After the initial shock of the first coat they smile and admire each other, happy now.

You are on the hinge of things. As the moments pass you find yourself in different places. The ground beneath you is as questionable as the direction of the breeze. If you were falling that at least would be a direction. This is different, like being suspended with the where changing at random. Your confusion is soft and spongy before you. You dig your fingernails into it and try to burrow. Perhaps things are becoming clearer as you dig a hole in your confusion and pull yourself into it. Are you passing through it? You peel back the covers on everything and still the vision from the top window lingers. You feel the dust of the sill upon your fingertips. The light is burnt with day. As you look down upon the neighborhood the world is silent and still. You cannot imagine asking anything further from it.

II. Within

The light extends from rounded objects, curvy as women. Light can hang from a chain in the numb frost of inside. Looking for the horizontal places inside. Walls can stare me down, old blank faces behind yellow breath. There are hiding places in the morning and at night where the chained light cannot reach and unhiding places when the house is empty. After a while I don't need the hiding places because he and momma can't see me. The house could be filled with fishes, swimming through the air between the rooms in bright colored schools, and they wouldn't know. It is—about the fishes I mean.

The windows are lying. There is no horizon and the world ends abruptly beige above too. The walls hold me in the bunched light, and only the rug red. Red like a ladder down, without rungs, into the liquid of it. Vines and palms, snaking through the red with the dull green illusion of surface, float there like that. The rug on the floor is a rectangle of wilderness.

I can't find you. I find you everywhere. The house stands between us as I watch you, the wheels of my skateboard turning within me. You stand before the window and I can't tell how old you are exactly. Your face is a floating impression on the bar of shadow upon the chair opposite me at breakfast. The contours of this trapped world are uncertain and I find myself crouching in the morning lights' frost against the wall, searching for you. Our touch is an heirloom of brass. At night a trumpet, each morning it awakens as brass. In these mornings I blame you for my poverty's whelp-pale face. You hide from me because each time I find you I scrub you hard with wishes. The hem of your skirt is the color of afternoons and you know it. I find you in the hall and I pass my hand over your forehead where it meets your brown hair. Freckled and foreign, your skin is a gummy little fanfare. I feel a longing for you and know that I have found a life within the trapped world. But I can't find you. We will never be introduced. Your heart is like the smell of cats. It swells in closets and thin air.

I am the butch boy you discover. I am small and thin and my hair is cut brutally. My head seems to bob on a pin above the tee-shirt. When there was an outside I felt people in the breezes. Now the day is a web of stairs and there is only you. Momma says I have the eyes of a seal. Sometimes I find you on the couch like a curled up past and I search within you for the shiny things.

The stairs are a ruffle you walk down. You are the young girl I find everywhere. You wear a plain dress but you seem excited as you rush into the kitchen. I only find pieces of you. As if I could paste you together with wood and glue, I gather the pieces in my arms. The trapped world is as hungry as the dirt. It holds us trembling, but I am just a boy with wood and glue wandering within it.

Time is a square flat panel between us like a membrane. Your heart is in the panel and the panel is a nest of veins that thickets with our touch. This act we call our touch, a headline on the bannister that snakes its way down into the murky red. Our insides glow with seeds and ribbed like melons we break open. The heart is the heart of the touch that forks like voices autumn colored which is what? I ask you and you crumble beneath the pressure of my lips.

Our touch then. Is there someone else in these hemispheres of lamplight? In the house alone at night I wait for your warmth. Our conversations are pinned to my breathing by sleep's intimate heaviness. In the silent darkness we whisper pedaling toward our touch. Brown hair brushed back, yes. Small round eyes like leather buttons, yes. The skin whose color is light and cold bath water, yes, and then? Then lost: holding my own hand as gravity's hammer splinters my ribs in the empty air. Our touch is just an advertisement.

Out of the butch boy's disappointment a picture of the girl begins to form. A name almost comes to him but of course this is too much to ask. The printed dress and the traces of a voice are enough. Here inside, where the sense has been wrung out of things, this reaching has become his native language. Momma and her husband are like statuettes that know when not to make a nuisance of themselves. The girl is a piece of dog-eared paper unfolding upon the window and letting the light that is a lie pass through it. The butch boy can see an outline and it is this that reinforces his dream of a solid world.

The voice is a little lower than he thought it would be, but just as pleasant. *Hello*, it says, *is there someone there?*

Yes, I say, *maybe*. Small bubbles slide along the inside of my head.

Well? she says. Here is the problem. The red *and*

then that turns over on its back exposing its belly, giving up.

But the butch boy approaches the quivering outline in the lying light to find the girl, and he finds her. Not his heart's trick. Not some smell upon the air. Not the window's invitation to the lie. He finds the girl and for a moment he holds her soft shoulders in his hands. The strangeness of the meeting refuses to strike him. You recognize me and we look at each other as you touch back. There is a confusion beginning. I find out that our touch is only an approximation. We slip into each other and the outlines are gone. I have found your mouth but now my only choice is whether or not to use it to talk. We spin up the stairs airborne, like two heavy objects on either end of a string. Which of us is left here, because there is a trapped world where fishes pass through the air in bright colored schools. There is a grandmother who cannot see the shed lives on the grass. There is place, a marker of something continuing out of the twirling and refusing to recognize movement. The immobile depth of place, having nothing to do with inches or miles but past years to something else that has to do with continuing past downfall and memory too, until all that is left is the grim and tireless echo of having taken up space.

So there we are upon the hinge of things. We feel a breeze upon our faces and we cannot step down to the same place twice. You see me and you wonder if you have become unsewn. Have the butch boy and his family moved away? When you tell me this I laugh. We pass out through the doorways like the sounds of breakfast and somewhere though he doesn't know it the butch boy is happy. The morning and its hinge of neighborhoods as you and I play in the pale green light of the house's past, and the summers last forever.

LAS MENINAS

Necessary Precursor of Silence

There were wire fences on either side. The light rose slowly on the wire-rimmed road. Its shallow-rutted mud, dried now, extended further between the trees. The unobtrusive figure of a middle-aged man in a brown coat disappeared slowly around a curve. There was a dark coming to the opening between the trees above the road. A cloud must have passed the sun's path, though it remained unseen because of the trees. There was a sense of gathering, not a storm exactly, but more as if the watch hand had slowed up, attracting things to itself, before it continued. That sensation that it was afternoon already and for the rest of the day. The air had cold in it, and just ahead the man's walking made quiet sounds. It was not yet nine o'clock in the morning. Disheveled and thin, the corduroy at the elbows of his jacket worn-through, the walking man appeared distracted and weary. Here and there vines had grown up in small bushes around the base of the trees and he turned his face toward them to try and find out what rustled there. Vaguely annoyed, he continued on his way slowly.

He moved without direction. A mass of black birds converged upon the high tip of a pine. Where the road stretched itself out could be seen the cut of the hillside in the muted brown of the dirt without any trace of sand and only small irregular areas of gravel to show what the road had been. Continuing to descend slightly, it came at times to spots where standing on a bulge of the hill one could see the entire small valley with its tucked houses and uniform green face. It was here that the man would stop for a moment and look across the land that refused to yield up its movement to him. He pulled a few pieces of paper from his coat pocket and sorted them out. He continued walking, looking at the papers carefully, absorbed in notes to himself or a letter from his daughter or who knows what. There was nothing attractive about the distinct smell of this morning or the blue and white markings of the bird that recomposed itself with each movement, there was only the added pressure of their complexity to him.

Something had been breaking forth for some time. It ran out ahead of him with all his strength in its belly. It began as a festival of thoughts and passions. Every day a booth with a smiling young person behind the counter handing out string. With each minute the string worked better, and all importance became a bundle which in turn became a single object.

The man walking thinks of looking for a place to lie down beneath the trees and be still. But he is fine. He is simply astonished at having a solid thing within him. He tries to make it rattle words. As the road before him where he could sing like a middle-aged man beneath the trees. As the flat tongue of dried mud coloring his shoes. As the color in his face and the height of things. As the changing wrought in the breeze almost here. As in any going from one place to another.

But the object has filled him completely and he knows that he will never speak another word again.

Ballista and Bassoon in March

Strung across on something, eight stones deeply scratched with some small metal thing. The child's eyes are as big as thumbs above a mentioned mouth. The woman's eyebrows are too dark: Isabel? This name perhaps on an envelope or hidden under the child's singing of a fidgety noise, turning it to strung stone. The child is serious. The woman's face is polishing. Laugh. Someone sleeping, this face pinched gentle. The rose and green of the beach blanket where it is folded changes the weather. The child's eyes at the end of two sticks as he is drumming as he is a bowlegged crab, red from sleep. Light bends strings over wood above wash between poles along singing like a sack of seed shook. The woman's grace is unfolding, the child has chicken legs, bowlegging in and about her. This is how. With the small aluminum doors of her, opening on hinges. The child sees his face in the mirror there. She wants. The overlapping sheets of paper on the desk make a disorderly star of rectangles. It has begun raining in the branches. It can be heard on the ground. March is a vague sound between clouds above our melody of heads and the small flowers popping in the branches from the rain. Everything is built of houses. Since feel means build and build means house. Houses in her face. The child turns round and round in his mask. The net of March is lifting, its few remaining days still in sight with their crossed harmonies. She raises her large clay hands, plants taking root and beginning to show in them, she raises them to the child whose body tips.

Attic

What does the child see from the window? He sees the hard wall of the night air. And there, the black areas without outline or volume. There are no mountains where the black remains. Suppose the mass of mountain range, fallen into the black shape and gone. And the passing shapes are black. Rubbing up against each other like thick paper. Intersecting black shapes hint at a path broken through the bottom of the night air. How many absences are moving in the dark. The child feels himself bisected by a giant blackness. He has imagined it in the shape of an iceberg, there where he lies halved on the wooden boards like a broken doll. He feels it tip within him. He imagines climbing it, one hand on either side. His legs are splayed out. At the window he hopes for the impossible colored birds to fill the black shapes that glide and eliminate the small lights. It is mostly black now. Maybe somewhere pulled along on a chain there is a small red car filled with yellow birds. He imagines the black shapes rumbling but they are silent.

Even though the child walks calmly down the middle of the street between paper trees, his head begins to roll away from his body in the attic, out the window like a rolling silver coin, antique somehow. A disconnected headlight is an empty bowl. The child's head rolls further. He lies upon the wooden boards reflected in an abandoned ornament whose green surface is coated with a thin film, from the air here, as well as the child's image. The child's head rolls from the black circle where the moon has fallen. There is a small paper dog whining to be let in beneath the porch light he has imagined. The child's head rolls further, like a lost ball between cars, his face still scrawled on it. From the window, his sadness pokes out like the beam of a flashlight.

Popa

Ask him why. Go ahead and see. Suspenders over his big and husky as he paces and see if I'm not mistaken. Nudge him. Give him a hammer and watch. Close the door behind him and be quiet; not to be cruel to him.

The streets are mud still. Houses on stilts. The hammer beats out the brains of starlings, that's how he hears the clacking. Everything is slowly minor. Popa carries a metal wash basin, leaving it somewhere, picking up something else again.

I have always loved fountains, Popa says. I have never wanted to pee in anyone's mouth, but it looks real nice with trees around it. This is a strange thought for someone sitting on a bench. I sit down with all the fittings and washers in front of me, it takes me awhile, but I finally make a workable mousetrap out of the makings of the faucet. It works like a guillotine, provided you keep the edge sharp. You see, Popa says, you see. When someone says leave me alone they mean it. Popa laughs. He is just a lamb with a broken rifle.

Where does Popa rest? On the water-stained leaves of an open book. In the thin aisles of the dark with the bulb swinging slowly from the rafters in the wet lean-to left to him by his departed. Popa has a german skull. In the nest of newspapers and the light green blanket that smells of. Popa's head peeks out bald with its brass temples forging sense as dislocated phrases pass up through the reading glasses. In this he is like the insectwoman in the center of the projects somewhere, her jaws dripping with nectar as they click. Her head however is encased at the top by a large crocheted sack, formless and larval. With his pursed lips and his rigid chest, Popa has been consumptive. It is as a dead man that he walks past his use.

When Popa collapses (Popa never rests) in the ruts of the mud, there is always the chance. Turned to pulp by the rain, Popa is denied the small explosion of feathers by which he has honored many a starling. The small bump of him left beneath the jacket in the road is as soft as his eyes in their red pockets gone.

Prod and poke, as I said. Your best Mister hey. Whispering medical talk. With the first warmth on the road, what was Popa gives off the smell of peaches. Billow an empty shirt. Mistake for whistling. Morning, go ahead. Pocket knife in the mud.

Apostrophe

Alone on a chair in the dark.

Two voices.

One circles the other.

See what I have found. Passing beneath the boughs of the apple orchard.

Ping, Clang, simple sounds, see. The air has snowed its petals and the gothic insects fill it now. I have been collecting things. I have not overlooked their small green bodies.

Autumn rain. Autumn mist. Hours with a basket. Braiding reeds and sparrows. Those words, where have I misplaced them? I saw bevel. Bevel and I misplaced each other. Simple sound. You can't invent bees. The twigs are in wax paper. The curtain softly.

Walking along the wet ground. Vines have climbed a tree. With their leaves like wooden flutes. A blue and thickish bottle beside a sand dollar warmed at the light. A leaf again, my sandals clacking. Breathing is an archeology. Gathering in the weeds. Finding a light brown pebble, the smooth egg of some small stream.

Ping.

Spreading out a blanket. I open the old book and read the word "genus" as I sit thinking of sleeping children and a spot of yellow at the base of a flower. Small shoes beneath glass, a deep ash box of needles and a silver thimble. Volumes of the cloth of centuries. Reading the word "brocade". My head in the shoots of grass, I remember "Noctuidae". "Catocala cara".

The chill has come in. It is time to put away the old book and what food I have brought with me. I refill the basket. The thought occurs to me to bury it. I decide against it. I place the folded blanket on top of its contents. It will be time for crickets and buttermilk moon in about an hour and no sign of my companion. I stand as still as a character in a book, reading: "She stands knowing something will happen soon."

Bells.

Bells.

Bells.

Something does. Something always does.

Epistrophe

Alone on a chair in the dark.

Two voices.

One remains stationary.

The word "church" has a bitter sound, sour unto being. Lingering in the word's vestibule before continuing.

Ash and still water. These are blankets. Find, and if I could have made an elemental house. The marble in the vestibule is an eye socket. It has risen from its interment. The autumn shadows are its polishing cloth.

Silenced in my pennywhistling by the two rows of pews. Stitch. That's what it sounds like. The voices perhaps hidden there in the joints of the pews like grease. Stitch, stitch. The candles lie cold. The smoke of their extinguishing has left its smell. The walls have greyed and appear jagged. Remember the color of the door.

The sound of sanding, hushing the lead birds chipped and fallen. The perimeter of the building drawn on a piece of paper is inexact, weightless. The fact is high and dark beyond designing. I have gone exploring in an empty church. Stitch. Some of the floor boards may have rotted away. A strand of light falls from a high window. Six point six two six two zero plus or minus zero point zero zero zero zero five times ten to the negative thirty-fourth joule- second.

Stitch.

I run to the altar and my boot clanks on the first step throughout the church. But this step is easy. This and the

73

next. They are two quick steps. Clank-clack. It is on the next two that I feel something akin to dread but deeper, making even fear seem not to the point. I tell myself I am not thinking of sacrilege, that in fact I am looking for somewhere to hide and feel encased. That the church drops words from the high windows. I am on the altar and look only quickly out at the pews before becoming frantic. For the moment I have forgotten the word "door". I look out again and am cold. Something gives way and I am in the small chamber with blue walls, with only the bell rope to keep me company.

I pull on it.

Bells.

Bells.

Bells.

Objects Connected by String
One and Two

ONE

The roofs of the village are made of slate. The color of elephants, though elephants are not to be spoken of here. The village has many wells. The days become cloudy by our looking at them. Say heavy, lead say. Remember the children's faces, whether austere or placid, behind high clean windows, a depth of shadow behind the small beige faces. Say cobbles, murmur, murmur toy shops with their polished wood and red paint. All the photographs have been murdered and there are only the village words. Not to be spoken of here. A group of birds circling in the air is recalled. There is a clock tower. Not to be forgotten.

There is a maker in the village. Some thought at first that he was a maker of birds. But, while amusing, this was not true. He came from a large city, some thought Vienna, but these things can never be verified. He cast metal in the shape of hats for giants and lilliputians. Bells. He made bells. He made more bells than Poe or chance. But what is chance but three men whose hats are too small deciding what direction to take.

The village was intrigued and the maker was old. If I could tell you what the people wore in this village, the olive green, the shades of grey and gold chain, the red as of a bell pepper, but I can't. When asked he confessed to making ninety-four bells. This was the number of years he thought he would live when he began his task as a boy.

Sometimes there were festivals in the village. Brightly colored vests etc.

But the bells. Yes, the bells, I am allowed to tell you about those. There were tinkle-tinkle bells, small and shiny and nervous, prone to gathering together and giggling. Large barnacled sea bells, intoning their solemn undertones and greening with big texture. Clanging middle sized bells that clamored among men and women, and could direct the traffic when they had a mind. Cow bells, goat bells, child bells, cloud bells. Is every tongue a mallet?

And this bell maker, how did he look? Like all bell makers, short, stooped, glasses with gold rims, a beard, always old by the time we notice him in his indistinct clothes.

Was he a sad old man? The village thought so.

And why was he making these bells? He made the bells that would ring at his death. The bell maker's life was a glass bell, and when it ceased sounding he would let the echoes escape its bonnet. He made a mechanism so that he might continue sounding. He rented an abandoned structure, perhaps an old cathedral made of stone, perhaps nothing so easy. He attached his ninety-four bells to the rafters, his ninety-four songs. To these he attached rope or twine as befitted the bell and made a web by attaching these strands to the floor. The web became as dense as a cocoon. When the bell maker felt his time had come he stepped into this cocoon and attached the last strands behind him. Was he weary? He imagined that in the next moments he would in fact die, and that his body would cause a great clamor as it fell. He imagined their coming at the noise, and finding him; and the music they would make, the song of his life, as they attempted to remove him from the web.

A few questions about the village. Was it near the sea? Were these inscrutable northern people? What did their old look like? This is often telling about a people. Did they resemble turtles or gulls? Small dogs or birds of prey? Were they like pebbles or sticks? Were they happy with the bells they had bought from the old man? Did they wear sweaters of a sunday? Were they peasants or merchants? Had the village had a height, or was it timeless? Had each heart become a peach pit, a clock gear; or were there blushing murmurs in the doorways in the evenings?

Here is the truth: it was three o'clock when he

realized he wouldn't die. He found his smallest movements created bell sounds. He began to choose his movements. It was as if all his work were at his fingertips. He
filled the village with his bell sentences. The bell maker
had become quite good at this by the time Marina arrived
with coffee for him in a small porcelain cup.

There are other questions to be answered. Did he
extract himself? If not, how did he eat? Is that it? etc. But
I remain unapologetic. This is all I will tell.

He didn't die until some time later, but in our mania
for the exact we cannot help but be frustrated by not
knowing when.

To say merely bell.

TWO

Poetry has the rare quality of making its vagaries
the portals to exact though diverse possibilities. Take the
lines,

> The birds perfume the woods
> The rocks their great nocturnal lakes

Eluard via Beckett. Now, not to concern ourselves
with the wonderous transformations of translation, let
us look at what has arrived. What do these lines convey.
We may ensnare ourselves in complications immediately.
Such as: The only birds who "perfume" anything are dead
birds. Or: They must be perfuming with movement. Therefore the perfume is its own delivery.

But let us follow a particular path and attempt to
find one or two simple possibilities of beauty behind the
foliage. Let us say the birds first perfume with their
color, and then with their sound.

The birds perfume the woods with their colors. The
deep blue of tropic waters. The yellow fleck upon the

wing. The startling orange beak. All this brought to the woods in the vessel of the bird, or more precisely its feathers. Dropping them, lining its nest with them, the bird does indeed perfume the woods with its feathers. With its mechanism for flight. The birds perfume the woods with flight.

From where do the birds bring these colors. Perhaps from "The rocks their nocturnal lakes". The rocks as reservoirs of color. They grow pale from use in the sunlight and only regain their hue at night. An imagined past when rocks were the color of birds. An ecology of pigment. Perhaps the rocks do not rejuvenate and we are witnessing the tragedy of the saltine cracker. The world is becoming washed out.

The birds perfume the woods with their sound. The chirping or squawking or falling notes are indeed inside them. A small flame of sound. Weaving the trunks of the trees with sound. Sound is as insidious as smell. The invisible perfume ringing in the trees. The heady sound of twilight.

And the rocks? Cage has said that at one point it occured to him that every object contained a sound within it waiting to be released. If so, then the stone contains the ultimate of these sounds. We spin about on the biggest rock we have, and we tap its sound to make all our sounds. The blank faces of the rocks are guardians of the resonance within.

The thought occurs that perhaps "The rocks their nocturnal lakes" modifies "the woods". In which case the woods and the rocks are the two elements which share a kinship. The birds are merely messengers, a baroque afterthought, with perfume as the continuing message between the rocks and trees. It is this thought that reunifies the elements as a stable image, and slips the words back into the fabric of the two lines, like sound into a stone.

(for elephant number one and
elephant number two)

Food and Beverage Management
in Hotels (Illus.)

Sam's fat hands found their way out of the monkey suit sleeves without noticing anything, not the ice bucket nor the light upon the grey building whose shafts are always ascending. A window on the north face closed, the stairway opened toward the bottom as the red rug widened, but there is nothing to pictures. Prepare something, say an infant's forehead for a mother's kiss, but every recipe needs numbers before the identity of that which is to be specified in type and size. Therefore, Sam is not enough. There are things which have nothing to do with Sam, and I am safe from all this, here on my cart. Monkeys at every light fixture. The beginning of the house of monkeys and I roll along on my cart immune from monkey shit and chattering and all Ben's rhetoric. Make a distinction and then sever the two things distinguished and you will see it is all the same brown stuff etc. Prepared etc. Sam lifts himself in his monkey suit in the dumbwaiter shaft, in his little elevator, hand over hand lifting himself up with the rope in his system etc. etc. Ben with his small glasses before him on the table, rubbing his eyes before replacing the wire-rimmed glasses. Ben with a chisel and at ease concentrating as he removes a bolt that has rusted solid. Ben fixing some clacking by installing a hum. His head stuck in something large and metallic. My cart passes four seated figures. They pass words between them and Molly says something tiresome that something is tiresome about a horse that did not deserve love. I am prepared to go through with this. Molly has a sad face and the others do not deserve names. They are two couples altogether though Molly is worth the attention they are all four thin and tall. They have God, do not be mistaken in this, and the shape of this is always random though high and preferably made of glass. My face is a bright metallic dome. My hands are tall

water glasses. Ben, my god, your face, you look awful.
Ben did not kill himself though I was scared he might,
though I haven't heard from him in ages his voice so fine
to hear would have made fine singing or has. Why must
everything change to animals and dark places when it
has been eaten, because everything has been eaten of
course of monkeys, I said Ben, please, enough with the
ladders and the monkeys. And he, but can't you smell the
fur everywhere, and their mouths like rubber cups trans-
form the building into a chest of drawers, homogeneous
articles on each floor. My cart is still fairly close to the
two couples, to the four seated wires with beads of water
masquerading down their stems. Molly, I hardly knew
you. Molly was a high fine myth and her voice hides in her
chin so holding itself charmingly dignified and girlish
before it begins to click. Sam carrying someone's bags
passes before her, his upper lip raised slightly over his
front teeth as he strains, no longer young and without the
small horns and hoofs of youth or anything. Think of me
as an organ grinder grinding myself transformed and
then all of us in the lights, swinging from our tails up
there in the molding and contsellations with organs of
our own, no longer having to borrow. Ben, enough. My
cart moves onward and I will be delivered. I lie upon a
white cloth that gently lifts, like a skirt, with the movement. The monkeys lift and toss each other along the
rafters like trapeze artists. My brain is in the shape of a
continent and my hair is mere parsley. Astoria is talking
so Molly shuts up. Astoria is bright and has money like
words on a piece of paper in the pocket of a bum. Crazy
religious stuff, money is. Complications lurking about,
Astoria says, too many spiders and eggheads to be sure.
See first illustration. See anything at all. How illustrious
her pearls are, strung together grasping and opaque from
her high throat. Behind her the custard yellow wall
unstained though she can hear the monkeys rubbing
against it. End of first illustration. See me disappearing
down the hall on my cart. Molly clicks but Astoria admits
to being an insect to Bob or Bill or Dan or Henry in his

fine formal posture resembling her, drink in hand, but not to Hank, there is no Hank here to speak of. The other two (of the four) remain faceless though well dressed. Astoria and Molly exchange glances, so that it is again Molly's earthiness within the polish that commands admiration sitting at her side. I pass it, commanded there on the rug like a lap dog and prone to the same mistakes, and mutter no I won't kill Ben even though I am prepared and Sam's arms are tired and the sleeve to his uniform has ripped with the effort and his greying hair peeks out from his cap. It is simply not in me. There are hump-backed people (Sam's wife, Ben, perhaps Sam himself) and hump-backed whales and one must not assume that since one is good the other must necessarily be good. See second illustration. The body is served up. The whole effect is comical if not conical etc. Every bed when uncovered is a tray etc. Ben calling long distance and the monkeys hanging from the wires. The connection and Sam diminishing etc. etc. If you fill a room with mirrors you empty it. End of second illustration. Much of the talk in and of the lobby is regarding palm trees and summering and their relation. One thinks of the monkeys and laughs at their creased fingers. My cart is passing a row of doors on either side as it hums along the carpet. Printed on the doors are the quantities of the recipe's ingredients in bright metal letters. Perhaps it is Sam who has my cart in his hands at this very moment and who guides me to my so called destination. I am prepared. Ben has fixed my cart many times, oiling, honing, with extraordinary patience for something so simple, as if he were putting the stars in their places. See third illustration. The switchboard operator claims she has fifty-four plugs and fiftythree holes. With so many holes plugged up this is only open to conjecture. She has been told she should consider herself lucky. She is overworked however and rarely has time to consider it. There are many designs in the rug that she has never noticed and perhaps she is in a private conspiracy with Sam's hands on this score. Admiration has left a warm wetness on Sam's socks. End of third illustration thank god. The monkeys form french curves and arabesques on the ceiling. I proceed warm and sanitary down the hall. My cart moves with a sense of purpose. To speak of sacrifices is preposterous since in the first place the word has always eluded me and in the second place I am no more than a bit of this and a scrap of that tastefully (I should hope) put together. In any case, rolling along smoothly is quite wonderful and when he or she who propels me, I almost called him or her my propeller, becomes animated, making the doorways blur past, it is almost inspiring. My cart moves along quietly toward the door at the end of the hall where my arrival is anxiously awaited. This is not an endless movement. My cart is straddled by the doorway as the door opens back before me. I am presented shining as I enter. I have arrived. My face is lifted. I wait to be undone. I am prepared. End of all illustrations.

Pages From the Lathe

I. Abstract With Mobile

A chain then. The maypole of our dangling. The crowded street heavy with ribbons within each head. The clocktower rises and its side yellow, sunned down but for the blue, beneath, where it has endured scratches. Some of the yellow thread in the full grey overcoats of the crowd. The street fans to points in different directions, the people, us here stepping out of its line as if over a white string. Walking, hand in pocket, bent at waist for further consideration of movement along. Fingers gently to the brim of hats as if they were childred's faces. The rustling of someone's coat sleeve against the wall of the theater speaks of a carelessness, of almost spring. There is no other place, leave this tiny square and step from the edge of the world into the stained black sheet that leaves its dye on your face and hands and drops its grains of sand into your mouth, onto your eyes.

The sidewalks are lower and flatter than remembered. Children whose hearts are red have wandered through doorways and mailslots. A woman weeps when she goes home and forgets to retrieve her little boy who surveys the pet shop and is pirate captain of the clothes store. At home alone she fears she has gone insane. In the clothes store he marshalls mannequins down below.

A chain then. No manner of lizards dressed for Sunday down below could justify the whole sky being a store window. Perhaps they are well-read little chickens and foxes leaving their pasty messes on the ledges. A chain nonetheless from behind the faded blue paper up top. The sky was darker once and the sun has slowly paled it? A chain down from the blue into the heart of wires. Steel rods passing out from the center about thirty to forty feet, like spiders' legs, ending in the mid-section of each dangling figure.

We bounce to and fro like punctuation to this explosion of metal. Once we were bulbs or lights and then we just grew here dangling above the crowd of well-mannered fishes mingling in the winter street.

Touch is our only suspiration and the wind and we live for it nonetheless. The colored lights from the clocktower at night and our lost faces on the hat rack high above. The tension at our lowest points is Icarian with music.

My fingertips brush another's and then we shed the brief grip that remains within us.

II. Lanternlight

I am a fox in a thicket, and to find me is to find the world lit with color. I curl down lemonhearted on a striped skirt abandoned by a poor woman in the green. My cross-eyed fury is burs and biscuits. The grey world blurs reddish. My teeth once found a singer's ankle. I watch as the birds splinter and my nose upon the ruddy stems.

The moon asked a clocktower if it would be cold tonight and the clocktower laughed.

* * *

Beneath its pearled ridges, the water is fibrous and dark. The bones of water make skeleton huts. I turn pale faces toward my resting place. The shudder of movement is cool even in the shallows now. I break off in all directions, hump out to many deaths in the single ringing. The world is deep with dark, even where the pearly bone caresses me. I fragment down beneath where I have found a drum. My children's wings are white and silent as they tear me open in the air. The rocks along the waterline are pecked to pieces by the wind. The creases in my hands channel the blood off my palms and down my arms.

My face is eyeless and it is dark as I am lifted into the shallows of the clouds by all the children clamoring in the world.

III. Small Town Incident Here

The small clown lifts one hand and then the other. He places one on either side of the sun. His face is thick and reddish, as is the sun's. His red and green conical hat is tipped forward on his head and a shoot of black hair slips out before it. The small clown is almost bald but is not drunk. He holds the sun and brings his face toward it. He purses his lips. His baggy sleeves ripple with the silent laughter in his chest. He places the sun on his head and begins to balance it there, exaggerating the movement in his knees, letting his hands slip out like shovels. He raises his eyebrows in expectation. He looks straight ahead. Then left. Then right. He smiles and stops. His hat is in his hand. He takes the sun once again between his palms. The make-up around his eyes is in the shape of stars. Ah-ha, he says and smiles again.

The small clown looks up at the sun. He attempts to let go of it but it begins to fall. He catches it and stands holding it again. He makes an expression of thinking over the problem.

He lets go of the sun and runs left. He reappears with a coatrack but has to abandon it to catch the sun before it sets completely. He lifts the sun and considers it and then the coatrack.

He tosses the sun up out of view and runs over to the coatrack. Retrieving it, he returns and waits. He looks up. Coatrack in hand, he continues to wait. Hours pass. He considers weeping, but continues to wait. The sun reappears just above his head. It remains stationary. The small clown places the coatrack beneath it. The sun remains stationary. The small clown waits. Then he replaces his conical hat on his head and steps out of view to the right.

The sun and coatrack remain. For some time.

IV. The Object Falls

Down—the fall like knees and necks on the steps until the hounds come sniffing. The great machinery is clacking, ever fond of its grinding down. If there were bells and tourniquets they would be in use. Hammered clicking, giving small resistance and then forward, like a bicycle. The engine in your chest goes down the steps like a child released. The dull blow on the face. The ferris lights in the cranial bucket. Hitting the ground. The small flower of dust around you. Continuing down. Your back arched, your broken fingers splayed, anticipating.

V. There Was A Terrible Fire

Look, there is no reason for this voices in the dark business, since the ship gave its innards to the birds. It lay there on the sand, broken at its middle. Its concrete bulk sent forth rusted steel rods into the air, bobbing from the wind and children's hands at the waterline. There is an inside to it, where its back was broken. A down in there, the salt cold crawling in the dark. There are children's faces in the sunlit holes. Crabs pass over the shattered floors. The colors seen through the holes are incredible greens.

The ship lies disemboweled on the sand. Children pass over it like crabs, and the water comes to eat it away. It has come upon its resting place with a great grinding and now is being washed to nothing.

On dark days, the person strolling in the evening will find it attempting to distinguish the sea from sky. It will seem like a massive grey foundation with shoots of metal sprouting from it. It will seem wide and fallen. More than ever it will imply a ruin. The sand around it is smooth and wet. On this close hot day the sky seems to be blurred, or a series of dull stains. Birds hover over the water's hushing sound.

The place is deserted. There is a cliff with a row of trees along its rim behind you. Steps cut out of the cliff. A clear sound of falling has found you on this beach. It hovers around your head, washing it. You pass over the contours of the ship and feel the extent to which you have been crippled. Perhaps the fall, perhaps something else. You lie resting, your face pressed to a slab of metal that is cool now that there is no sun. Should you wait for the dome of stars and the moment of wonder? You decide against it and begin to move again. You find one of the holes the children stick their heads through. You begin to lower yourself down into it, down until you drop and land on something in the dark. Here you will lie suspended forever. Here you may disintegrate in peace.

Things continue moving.

Incendiary

A small wooden block and all the grey. The dark within the rectangle of a window frame and someone's face as they turn to speak the same color as a stained wall. Grasped at the ankles by the first figure's hands, the second figure grows out unhinged like a star of David flat up upon the first's shoulders. Small hooks, reminded of hands, refuse to move any longer except to imply tension at once lost in a small green tackle box of metal rusted at one corner with buckles on its face. Magnificent wheels please continue to turn upon one another flush at your rims and open at your centers to the breeze and the child would-be acrobats, with faces like paper plates, singing the music they continue to imagine within wheels, within rings. Every desert has irritated a moon from its coarse skin. How the domes of buildings fall from it! The second figure rises slightly like a pair of scissors. All glass is stained as is the light passing through it. Fruits become the shapes of the letters they begin with and there is something somber in this because all soldiers lie dead among the letters in the mud beneath the trees. Laughter rotting within a few words like a seed in the cracked helmet like an avocado in the grass. The fallen rifle upon the spread legs has finished the description of the letter A in green and black.

Direct

Clip and some. Must still silver. Joy high. Clouds. And then the line goes slicing, then the pressure down, the medal and myopic scholar, the steamer's steam made waving, first the hands were down then raised then down, a shoulder is a cam.

Clear. Needlejoining light. Lightly. Under the cold god's face. Simple was. Simple grill mimic mist down alone the was. In the sloping country, where the gentle spots of milklight, drawing up and bar hard, slipped the threads that small and nestled said green shawl the needle pick.

What of roll bone timid. Well again a silver faun by the cold tuned. Dirt. Light bark winged hazels are the earliest to bloom. The tree still grey blossoms silver bowl. Scholar's scarf. Grey stone tonic tip yellow steps. Spring pale white trunks dream-wing radiance filled weeks of dying once they have begun to confess how untruthful they become. As I saw the sun. Time has vanished. Weary in the darkness reddish glow the fish blue grotto. Bare trees so gently bleeds the humble. Arise walk toward step before forearm ascend bone and fat. Obedient unto. The sky is your hat. Breath. Hull. Pure candles' realm of roots. Voice that well tip consoling us. Man and tree.

Hawksaw. Rung. Pavilion hill top. Cutting all the dogs saw, mumbling and will, call and rerespond spending small the gull's heads, worrying. Again the will undo will wed. Flower plates the end hop, end blossom. Stall. Dark partition. Certain mid mere. Cleared. I fight the obscurity of the trees. Exalt. Unfasten. Tack down. Summer since it would have been of raising talk in branches was what of gone halt lingering without watching hinges as come up lifting. Gist ratchet. Escapement.

Perihedron

All round, about, beyond. The roofs hold. A crown unfolding, the sky bevels. The voice rises higher into the shattered air. Proclamations, like small vehicles, sheath the unimportance that is words. Words are falling from the tree of voice. The light pedals at its branches.

It is a seduction, this wanting to take a pistol and walk up to someone on the street and shoot him in the head. The apex of oranges and its king whispering for importance to gather. The great trunk and its unknown crown resounding. An iron softly smooths with pressure, the heat lies in the calculations.

First, the attempt to place an empty bottle and a paddle wheel above the pointed roofs. Will the erased and still dusty blue board hold such things. Imagine merely the bottle and the paddle wheel. This leaning back, eyes closed, pressing the trigger again. The coat worn, the expression. The bottle is perfect. The paddle wheel touches everything with complexity. Pah, that sound, pah. The paddle wheel with one broken paddle is yet never still. Never to step forward with loud footsteps. Inner music ferments in concentration. All round, about, beyond. The bottle is impenetrably shut, finished.

Beside the Paper Tree

Grief like slow water in its immense moving. A small room of people sitting in chairs, without sleep. Walking, I chanced to see the bottom of a sign missing, as if bitten off by something as it passed. The voices tearing at themselves. Sitting in my chair listening. Following it easiest when it was dark without sleep and the quiet was like a box whose sides fell away. It was not morbid in the least, it was not a coffin or a coffer, though accidents happen on the road. It was merely something to chase through the night air at my leisure. Because everything that could have said thing-thing was gone. I followed it lost. An old man sniffing at something beneath the trees. Jacob, come in now, my wife's voice called to me from the porch. I had stood on the porch that morning, looking out. I had seen that everything was dead. There are no words for this grief. I bless the silence and try to renew my faith that there is a skeleton beneath human flesh. Evenings spent walking. Days spent learning the rules of leaves and petals. Imagining a hand. There are insects made of groups of shells. Looking at my hand in its stupidity. My wife says that if I did not have blue eyes I would have made them up. I have certainly imagined strangers with a kind word who are gone now. In it I place whatever worth I may have tried to lift. I have not made what I have followed. I have not imagined or known it. I have lost us all. I have even tried to protect my grief. It leaves me slowly and I cannot conceive of further territories. Snow fell for a few moments at midday and then stopped inexplicably.

Carl's World

The amazing thing is that light can be pushed. It can exist in a substance, and that substance can be touched and prodded. It can be maneuvered in shapes to come around the head of a girl, to lay the sunlight there upon her forehead and face. A coat of light.

And yet light is a living moving thing. It tilts over the place where I stand like a slow pendulum. There are sources of light there and there and then everything is reflection. Light moves.

Here I stand in the garden. My name is Carl. My feet are in black rubber boots. My face is any face that is a man's face. It is a bright day. My hands hang at my sides as I look around me. My back aches and so I have stopped for a moment. I bend down again. The wheelbarrow is almost full with rocks. The garden is coming along.

It is not a big garden by any means, stretching as it does between the house and the garage. Its flower bushes are up and through the white fence that encloses it. The fence is not a picket fence. It runs along the inner edge of the sidewalk, from the house to the garage. There is another fence behind where I am standing to whoever has the next yard, but it is indiscriminate and high and things end there. The garden is roughly square and has rose and other flower bushes rising up on little mounds along its perimeter. In its middle I make straight rows and try different vegetables, gotten sometimes from friends and others from a gardening store nearby. This garden gets plenty of sun, being back here where it is, open and on display almost.

The house where we live is on a corner. It wouldn't mean anything to anybody if I were to name the streets. Just some corner, that's how I think of it. We live in the back half of the house and our landlord who is older and keeps to himself lives in the front. Our doorway faces the side of the garage. The garage empties out onto the side street. This is where everything is.

The house has all kinds of windows but still is dark somehow. I try to stay out in the open. To me, the house is too full of things. I like the garden because the garden breathes. In the house every counter and drawer seems like a place to sleep.

The garage is not ours to use. I park my car on the side street. The landlord parks his car in the garage. He lets me keep my tools there. There are steps up to the top part of the garage that has been made into a loft.

My wife left me. She sat at the table and looked across the room. She is a very nervous woman and I worried about her as she packed the car. She cries often and needs to move. People say, "Carl, oh yes Carl, Carl is a good guy." She calls me at times now and we laugh talking. She is a fine woman and still lives in town somewhere.

There is a young woman, a kid really, who rents the loft in the garage. She doesn't live there, she just visits there. Sometimes you can see the light on at all hours. I wonder sometimes what it is she does up there. She parks her car right behind mine. I don't talk to her because I figure it's none of my business. It's not as if I don't have things to attend to.

Light is fastening to things. Catching on the surface of objects in its path. It is a current that renders everything stationary by contrast. Coming to the tall bushes and fastening itself there for a moment touching before slipping off and continuing. Continuing out. The grey street pales and the bushes grow dusty. The shake roof on the garage seems to glisten. Light is not a heaviness or a lightness so much as a polish. Whether turned heavy or light by that touch, everything beneath the light is reordered. The light holds and holds still, a falling bandage. Bathing the small me beating here within it stationary. Light ornaments these shapes with its slip-falling. I toss another rock in the wheelbarrow and feel myself unbending in light again. As if I float in this movement that is just the slow getting used to it. I move slowly over the floor of the garden. I make a space away from the light, beneath me as I go. With the hours I feel the light on my back paling the shirt there, wearing with passage. The red patch of curtain in the kitchen window, I watch it out of the corner of my eye as I work. I watch it stay there, staying red and staying bright too. It touches the light back. I maneuver as I move so that it remains flashing in the corner of everything and the light is pollenating.

I am a janitor. I work at the hospital. I am not a custodian. I know what I do. Other people notice the clean halls sparkling where I notice the dull surface immobile drawing a human film to it. I ride the bus to work, and most of the time I get a ride home. It's not far. I walk it sometimes, deciding whether it is better to have a system or not. I have one when it occurs to me to think about it. I try not to hold my breath when I'm at work. Each job and the order they are to be done. The hospital is a territory I discover even though I pass over it every night. Palaces.

The child is dying. In the dark of the house, where he is the only thing living. I pass my hand over his forehead and he looks at me. Nothing the hospital can do. I stay in the house for him. He lies on the pink sofa, humming tunes to pass the time. He always has enough blankets. The furniture in the house gathers around him. I hover in the house and his voice. My wife Peggy won't speak about him over the phone and I don't ask her to. The child has small hands. He can't sleep unless I've got a fire going. The sofa is across the room from the fireplace. Otherwise he remains awake. We talk to each other as if something is going to happen soon.

I'm in the garage putting things away. I look at the stairs to the loft. She is not up there because her car isn't on the street and the garage is silent. I finish hanging things up on their pegs. I am at the stairs and walking up them. I flip open the door in the floor of the loft and pause to listen at nothing before poking my head through.

I put my head through and am underwater. The light came apart. I came up the rest of the steps. It is warm here. The light rises on panels and substance comes apart. It pressed on everything of me in that tank. I say some word and then I close my eyes. I was still there and the smell of the paint brings the light within my face and brain there too. My eyes are either opened or closed but my sight moves about the tank of light. Then I tried to think. I ran my fingers over the surfaces. Thinking: think. I become smaller, and nothing here but paint on something where light comes off of it. I became smaller and was outside in the yard without believing I am here or in outside still standing and about to enter the house and the child's supper and his dying.

You take the big logs first because those are the important ones. Two or three only. It's there that you guess the rough shape. Usually pyramided up into the corner since this is easier and works better than a tepee or a box. Then you begin to figure the path. A series of spaces for the kindling to burn out of and the air to chase itself through. Even with the kindling all in, there has to be enough space to get it going. The smaller logs should break in around the big one like ribs around a spine. The child looks over. The flame takes right away and needs no nursing this time because you have just cleaned the fireplace the night before. I sit in a chair watching the child sleep. This is the only time I like being in the house. The flame uses the ladder I have made for it.

Peggy sits at the kitchen table looking across the room. Her arm rests on the surface of the table from her elbow to her wrist. Her face is turned away from the cup of coffee before her as if she has forgotten it. She is motionless. Most of all her eyes. When she is about to move or when she has stopped for good it is always in her eyes first. Her eyes are heavy and not pointing at anything. She sits at the table almost touched by morning and I am already walking, humming to myself a few blocks away.

I rise up to the studio again. The paintings press against my sense of something happening. I would say blue and green because these are words that mean undersea, though the paintings are not these colors but more

often shades of yellow, white, and brown. I return up the
steps again. I go into the garage and up to the loft. It is
a small room with two windows feeding, or off of, light.
The walls on two sides slide open and contain dark
storage places. The paintings are stacked against all four
walls, so the smell. I leave the garden and enter the
garage, begin up the stairs and put my hand on the trap
door that flips up into the studio. There are jars and
tubes and the high rectangles where the contents have
flattened out almost, carrying things. Small ridges touching half a color with another and topography of blindness
and no more directions. The lowest step on the stairs to
the loft is broken nearly in half and gives a little too much
when I step on it. I open the side door to the garage
knowing she isn't up there before I enter. The stain that
is there begins to open up red in my throat and hounds my
head.

Here, the outside has come here and opened up its
belly. Now the outside is gone and I am the only moving
thing here in the world. The panels of color have closed
behind me and the dingy rugs have become counter-
weights to vibrancy. I am still standing and not suspended because of the dust rising from them. The cans
full of pencils and brushes are anemones and there is
nowhere to go, having come up these stairs there is
nothing left to do. This makes now dangerous. Cutting
myself away from this density again and again with less
success each time I move and displace light. The dust
rising shows me how solid the light between its flecks
remains. Pigment can become warmth and the smell of
alcohol. I can't make a list of colors, I can't find an order
to them just lipping up to each other. Yellow finds an
avenue, a crack or river. Yellow, the color at the center
that has split itself open where green and brown, though
with less force, converge on it. Yellow opening like a shell
around its white gut. One instance that has comman-
deered the other walls of light as if they were mirrors.
The wick of yellow reflected to the center of the room.
Removing my spine from it where it has left its imprint.

My movement brings about others and the balance of color changes and everything is overgrown with vines covering the walls as snakes around light and darkening the ceiling where red has begun to burn the green, changing it. There is nowhere to go and no way to watch. Light destroys me as it always comes down and out. The immobility is becoming complete. There is no hiding a statue when the world turns new. Describe any shape and I am in trouble without trying to describe it I cut it out of the light reducing me. There is nowhere to go. Light begins to move in and my hand glows orange up to it, my eyelids, my mouth.

The sound of her car and the engine turning off. The sound of her opening the side door to the garage. Her feet on the steps.

I have crawled into a storage area and closed the sliding door behind me. I sit in the darkness of the small space listening to her moving about in the studio. She is humming to herself, moving things around. I keep my breathing even and quiet. I don't move. At first the darkness is like a bee or a mask, just something hovering close to my face, getting in the way. Then it begins to move out over the plane of my face, a dark stone slate deepening, revealing the small lint lines of light still upon my eyes. Silent, I sit with my face pressed up into the dark. My slight movements I can only guess at. Sitting within a cool smooth jug, my inhaling slowly pulling shapes into my mouth. I am not in the bottom of something, I am in the crown of a building. I am pressing at the inside of the top of its skull. I am only guessing at where I am. Maybe somewhere in the dark of the child's breathing filled with unseen forks and spoons. I can only guess at my shape. I am not sleepy. There is dust and some smells here somewhere. Trying to remember the look of the paintings, but I can't, like trying to make up old bones. I listen for her and hear something miles away. When will I know if she's gone. I won't. The dark is an arrow suggesting itself. Keep the breathing quiet and slip into the muscles relaxing into the bottom of a sack.

My face is upturned but remains untouched. I don't feel anxious but more like powder in water. I open my eyes and close them. There is slightly more light when they are closed. My face is upturned as if I am sunning myself with darkness. I feel hollow and imagine my arms filling with dark water. My heart bends in then out somewhere in my imagined chest. A wreath of something hovers around my ears, making them ring. I brush up against things I don't know anything about. I sit inside my head and think briefly about spiders. I tingle in the dark along my legs and neck like a bag of spiders. My eyes remain closed. My head is in my hands. There is a large round object in my hands. I am turning it over, feeling the soft contours on the tips of my fingers. I am the light in the veins softly pulsing from some heart of things in the dark, bent in then out in the dark, pushing light away from itself and into the eyelids and legs growing out from it like slow rivers of mud. I am caking out more of myself, stuck and then after a moment slipping further out to where. To fill all the dark in the sock and the face and this here where the only sounds are muffled. Then I become solid as a brick with nothing around it. A single piece of stone propped up cold. Holding there without breath. Stuck and without insides. At the center of everything imagined out around it. Without waiting or sound. In the middle of something that could be anywhere because it will never crack open. Still. And then becoming flesh again. First a hum, and then a feverishness making the floor feel and the air full of things. Sitting there without place single for how long. Opening my eyes to find lines of light describing the edges of the door. Lines of light cutting straight across nothing until nothing begins to fill in with dark shapes around me. Shapes that with only outline seem like places to go. These shapes huddle around me. I could easily fall into one of them. I look again at the lines like the shape of some doorway fooling me into another darkness. I listen and the dark around me inhales. I listen and the shapes crowd around me humming, touching my arms. I listen and make up what

I hear. I listen and the floor begins to fall away beneath me. I put my fingers into the line of light, the crack in the door. I pull it across and everything comes in or out at once and I can't see and I listen and hope.

I ran down the stairs and out into the garden. Moving the painting leaning against the door I looked around the studio and quietly slipped out from behind the door. I didn't see a thing and suddenly I was outside. Looking one way and then the other I left the studio that looked exactly as when I came. What she had touched was back where it was before. I tripped and fell over something before flipping the trap door up and scrambling down the stairs. I couldn't see a thing, not the rugs, not the paintings and I made my way by touch. Feeling each stair with one foot first. I was scared she might still be in the garage beneath me and I stood without moving in the middle of the studio, listening. I broke the bottom stair as I came down without thinking putting all my weight on it not feeling anything as it snapped. Here I stand in the garden.

Carl stands still in the garden. Frozen there rumpled. He has been filling the wheelbarrow with rocks and he stops for a moment. The moment holds as the baggy man stands still for a moment in the garden. He is calm and graceful. Not somebody running holding his head full of bees in his hands as he runs. He is trapped by his grace into one moment. His feet are in black rubber boots. His jeans and shirt have been paled by wear and sunlight. The house's color presses up against his outline. Up to about his knees can be seen the brown of the dirt behind him. It is taken over by the pale green of last year's garden further up. Where the green meets the brown it has been flattened out so that the perspective is lost in favor of texture. The color used for his face and arms is unspeakable. Upon the simple lined face there is an area touched by light. Here it is impossible to tell whether the artist has abandoned realism or not. The side of the face where the light touches it seems perhaps a bit too humble beneath the baseball cap.

The Fifth Season

Our mouths are full. No. No. There is always something added later. The place lay at the bottom of a slope of apple trees, between this slope and a slightly humped plain which, while lined closely by these same broad grey voices that rose and branched like wood smoke and like it denied the silence by occupying it, seemed more open beneath the sky because one did not feel the need to rise through them first to rise at all but rather rose alongside them. My green I looked up through. My room in shadow drawn aside like a painting on a curtain. In this way it could be said that the place was between two legs of land, since the area in front and behind it had been cleared for the garden and various other uses; and the contour of the plain did resemble the inside of a thigh. No.

Words are the bent filament of fire, the implacable light. Poor water, in a barrel, its transparency in shadow. Leaf and tongue. There are no resemblances, my touched green, when you curled like the fingers around a rope, when you filled my nose and lungs in the August of collapsing. Old Julian's shape could be made out after a few moments where he stood before the door that he had just closed, waiting there in the quiet before continuing down the hall. The season plumpkined the fruit with orange light in the afternoons, beetling down the branches so that the trees seemed to explode and open like hands. The green skin of an apple over the ribs of a man. Gossip.

Enough. The russet dusk spoken of the orchard and slight tip to the ground are tender to one another. Martin, your sorrow. Look at the many elbows in each arm of the trees. Turn away. Their awe, in abundant bundles, cannot stop bending up. Thistle tipped. A leaf fever whose majesty. Martin delirium. I saw a hawk toying with the empty air and the next moment a sky of green leaves and tentacles. Within curtains and my good wishes, protected from such order, you won't see me again Martin. My eyes have been clouded over, like water muddied by movement, by the grace on the things of this world, their smallest chambers. The fire of looking, the over-turned bowl of listening. Thunderbolt, how many words did I teach you before you learned to fall and open upon the head of the world. No.

Belong to the breeze? Summer dragonfly, in your jaw your armor lives on undisguised. No Julian, you're right, I haven't learned a thing. My buzzing voice pre-pares its wing, gives its sigh; enunciates my debt, pulling it in. I heard a man running through the orchard. I curled away from his sound and was among the trees in birdless silence. William down, I am further troubled by my sound. An end to such annunciations. Shroud.

The trees are walking. Is there something sinister in stumbling. The young man runs into the garden and falling upon the rows begins to fill his mouth with earth. Another form of taking by infirmity, youth. He fills his nose and ears and eyes. Hands. The air is full of things because my thinking is a spider. He squirms and begins to gag on his nostalgia. Going I. A simple cell, its walls within plants, my greed is there. I will not take his glass head from him. The insects there inside. Words are the currency of nourishment and light. The orchard darkens and the birds are transfigured. This one touched by color upon the crown, the other a fleck of red upon the wing. Draw the small curtain of desire back. Still. A meteor is there.

I saw the mathematical reaches of the arteries. The branches risen to their buds. Lived, greened. The awak-ened pulse of the sun as it spoke in long sentences, pulling the rope of moisture as everything attempted to hold on and was grown. I gave my eyes of order to the world and then understood that they weren't mine to give. And yet the babbling continued, babbling blossoms and birds and berries as the days evaporated. Separate from it, I saw the many sided balance in it and tried to catch it in my hand. Because I thought it stood apart from time, from life. Then. There came an autumn, tongues tangled, devouring. The wind and I filled our bellies with it and lied to all the falling things. I will never forget being a knife, moving with such ease. The hand that must displace the air, that cannot leave. Turn with time. A cloud of mosquitos without water beneath it, without the reflection from which to take. Forgive me, William. At the tips of this movement, in the blood of seasons, I came here.

Grace has no reflection. There is only the conversation between the birds and their shadows, a change of light. What moves underside the branches reddening the silence. Holds the voices on the stretch of land, still. The air wouldn't hang a leaf. I walk toward a tree, its height removes the light. I have spent its protection. The ground, turned over, sparks its dead grass down. My mouth is always full of air, words waiting. But a pear is an old woman's ankle. A muscle is the color of an apple, in the eye of the ground. To say a mouth filled with insects is no reflection. William, take my weight.

A ball began rolling for no reason and then it stopped. Its voice has ceased breathing. Not to take again to fill my mouth. A mosquito lowers itself to the water's surface for food and a mosquito of light rises from the depth to give it. I stand here at the boundary where Martin fell. Blood is a small wheel on which touch turns us. The trees were as still as coral in the liquid lie. Julian and I carried him to his bed. The sun uses its pole of light to vault over the earth.

We follow. The trees believe in us and break us like kindling. They have no habits, the crowns are the right height and the light knows. Speaking in the air. The rows down the slope sift for the patches of dry grass and hold too. Martin, the others are troubled. They become invisible, some opaque and some transparent. Those that have soured open, rotted hand, stutter there like fallen dancers. Of harder substance is the blossom that eats us. Like someone standing on her hands, the green skirt's mysterious leaves and stillness. Birds show themselves merely by moving.

Divisible from what. Leaves look their own falling.

We could not carve, the ground gives. Green grown away, the bird bisects, hammocking for a moment before the black wings and body rise to face and cup back movement. Still the lead voices shape and hold green leaving. The small shadow fidgets, withdraws its wings. Light cannot fall past the ground. The stopped stream curls around voices in the air, leaves the branch skin fruit skin face skin of leaves bright before it is swallowed. My silence will be a gift whose wrapping, at least, will not be petty. No.

No. Give, a handful of rabbit dies close to me. I grow blind in the festival of blossoms, closer what is dropped wet still gets within my breath outlying. Its rustle won't wait in this small clearing. The grass is beaded. Dead means slanted down somehow. Shadow lids with petals, justices by taking, lies there. A single knock, a turned crown on the darkened wood. I looked back and it had gone.

The first leg stands, the second leg a stick beneath my limbs to bear movement.

Henry

Sewn into the lining of silence. Henry is budding, he waits quietly in hell for his name to be called. It is as silent as a pocket. His hair, as in life, is cut close on the sides of his head and a bit too long at the top, so that he looks like a finch. He has crawled up out of something useful. He is in his fifties, if this is important, and is dressed very much like a businessman of his time and city. He was my brother. My name is Louise, and I am not there to comfort him. If asked, Henry would say the room smells like phosphorus, something only partly known to him. The walls of course are red, of some hewn rock that gives off moisture, vaguely reminding Henry of caves he visited somewhere in Europe. That he cannot remember where annoys him. Nothing can be heard, I insist on this. Come out of many kinds of wood, at first only slowly and in relief, this is Henry; dampened by the very air but solid. He knows of course that he is dead, but rather than horrified he remains distracted. He is waiting quietly in hell, refreshed and expectant but aware of complications.

There are no dreams and this is just a railway station underground, very much like that, however Henry is dead and in hell and the day is getting on for him and he is tired. It has become apparent that his name will not be called today and he decides to go looking for a room. Yes, yes say all that again, his cutting his own throat, our grandfather's pearl handled razor, his child Louise finding him and screaming, jumping up and down strangely and falling on the tiles next to the body, her mother having to clean the blood from the child's clothes and then call me, but none of this interests me in the least. The elevator is broken and Henry must use the stairs.

There was still a trace of cold in the air. It seemed at this hour to gather around the village in small bundles like vespers. To be a young man in these hills, watching the carts cut across the face of the day as they came down the road from the hills and into the village. To joke with the old man driving it, his features having come to resemble the ox pulling him. You could see these young men walking along the roads in the morning, returning to their homes after having slept in the fields. To be drunk mostly with dreaming, lying under the stars, under the fabric of silence with the crickets and thoughts of women and leaving. To be tired with all this energy, to spend the evenings languishing about in front of the doorways. These young men were these hills.

Henry stands there, as if he had just come off the bus from the neighboring village, admiring the outskirts and feeling the cold breeze. He remade again his dream of a few quiet days and yet at the same time thought of how these things could drag on. The dusk made him melancholy and difficult, and he smiled thinking how out of place his moods were in this small village. Henry picked up his bags and entered the village. The small streets were lined with old buildings. Grey, no longer respecting the paint they had once been given, they were faceless to him.

And yet they were still touched by the light that brings insects. He could not help but understand their crumbling. Henry's arrival in the village was a paradox. His walking along the outskirts was peculiar, he seemed to be entering the village and hesitating, turning back, at the same time. Insects were baroque here. Henry was exploring the outskirts as if the word *skirts* were to be believed; he was feeling the broadcloth of the village between his fingers. At one corner he came upon a group of boys throwing stones at a chicken, killing it with large stones. Henry asked one of them, a tall boy, which was the best hotel in the village. The child took his bags and they began walking. The noises of the street were muted, as if they had a collar on.

Henry, I am expected at the grave sometime soon. The elevator will be full of men named Bob. I am expected with indulgence. Henry. The cab driver won't drive there directly since to him grief is a form of tourism. At the counter of the hotel Henry is startled. The old man

GEORGE ANGEL

behind it screamed at him. He tugged on a beaten green vest and came out around the counter. His hands were trembling and his old face looked wild and lost. Henry remembered how tired he was as he watched the old man approach him. How sad Henry looks waiting for the old man to come at him. How destroyed you have become. Henry gave his tenderness to the silent birds. The old man steps past him and through an open door behind Henry. He turns, watching the old man begin a furious argument with a group of men in an adjoining room. Henry was swept aside for some sort of village meeting. The arguments had gone on for hours before Henry had been allowed to check in. Henry is in hell. All my words have turned to thistles. To be brushed away. To sink the sea with fishes. Henry had asked the tall boy his name. The tall boy had wondered what Henry was used for, where he came from. He told Henry his name was Solomon, that it wasn't much further to the hotel. Henry waited for the silence of the boy's sandals, for the silence of time becoming thin and brittle to reassert that nothing was happening. He waited for the scent of some flower to develop, he unpacked his bags now in his room and thought of the sign in front of the hotel. People were arguing somewhere else. The sign had a black background and distinct yellow letters that said merely *hotel*. As he looked from it to the rows of windows rising, it seemed as if the cracks in the face of the building rose with his gaze, green from something growing in them. The vines of heat strangle all the buildings in this city. As I look out my window, I see the buildings leaning toward each other in suffocation. The cars along the broad avenues are suffocating. Everyone walking holds their breath. My voice sticks to my lungs and I will never leave this building.

I envy you. Henry you are much better off in your village. Have a drink downstairs in the bar!

Jingle jackal julep under ringing light to mingle out ill and under from the old man's banks from pills and plunder to the cold water's hand pulling under as the jackal swims away from mother. Drink, the dirty little trick. Henry sits with it in hand. It is as if every object has a light bulb in it, with as little grace as that. A few sad notes written on the back of an envelope. The eternally present early evening of the bar. Henry looks at the object in question and it is midased glowing. Bent at elbow fell withering in his own smell the young jackal unboned lifting groaned what was sung into the chair brung up tinkling glass as if he owned words but turned his own eyes to oysters in their monied shells. Henry sees the world in bow ties quietly excusing itself word by word from him. Glass has made light something to be bartered for balance. The hotel is so comfortable that Henry is weary and waits for the stick to drop sleep before his eyes. Beneath thrashing above washing a jackal pup is drowned beneath sound its teeth showing swimming its way at shadows bound by what it sees sinking. Henry sat dead into the evening. The little drink no longer gives good weight. Henry was uniformly thinning into the flat hour of continuing to watch things move. Suspended by liquid stiff as any unsuspended lost bundle soaked with the old man's watch chain catching the light just above the hands the jackal turns enduring its own night its own dissolving. A drink sits on the bar unattended.

My window is a flat black place. How to talk of the passage of Henry's night. He lies flat beneath lawn that was already mown when it was laid in cut squares on top of him, now among crickets and the shades of cold the night prepares in the cemeteries outside the city. The loneliness of his immaculate blankets. The silence of the box. The actuality of sprinklers or the fear of being outside at night in the open dark. The hole dug was not deep enough to escape darkness and only makes it worse. The bar is deserted and Henry is not feeling anything and has not felt anything. Memory lifts from him like adhesive tape. Henry is not anything but the time passing. Ask me but I cannot make him do anything more in the bar. I am unable even to return him to the room and bed he has rented. All I have for you is me in my apartment waiting out the clock and the blackness in the window. This will have to do, this will have to be Henry's first night in hell.

It was a difficult morning. Henry sat quietly with his coffee at a table in one corner of the small plaza. The village was running its machinery of bodies moving with their loads from one side of the square to the other. It was indistinct and bright to Henry, this slow movement within the day's expectations. It seemed staged for him. He thought again what little use his way of seeing things was to him here. He felt as if now he might be returning, that the worst was over. No justification for this feeling could be found and if he was returning, he had to admit that it was as a broken man. This cracking was what made him finally stand up, pay for his coffee, and return to the many mansions. It was worse there of course. Hell was much busier than he had left it. When time was found for him, Henry was interviewed several times, he was given forms. The clerks were tireless but cheerful. Henry found it charming, the whole business. It seemed hell was still a cottage industry, that it had never left the caverns. The surroundings struck him as beautiful; as if he were waiting in lines, giving his excuses at counters, using the complimentary pencil on line C, all inside an enormous chiselled stone head. The red of the moist silence made it seem as if we were all blushing. Henry felt there might be something here, a position perhaps. When they had exhausted him they told him of course that no more names would be called for the next few days. He left the great hall of hell reluctantly.

Once, in his office, Henry told me that he had never had a chance with those his age. Their, and perhaps his, tragedy was lost to him. They had turned themselves into titans of memory and downfall. They moved through constellations of betrayals that Henry could not find in his own life. He felt small beside them. Middle age was their great playing field while to Henry it was merely Wednesday. This had made him mysterious to his colleagues. They had never seen Henry filling the ears of younger men in the inspired and compulsive way they had. Worse yet, he could not even find it within him to take his coevals seriously. He saw each of them in his mind, wrapped in a bath towel and crowned by laurel leaves, leaving the bathroom and walking bravely toward sexual apotheosis. And the rhetoric and reminiscence it took to turn this into philosophy was a tempest. Henry had no stomach for it and remained decidedly unheroic. Instead he seemed to be slowly wearing away.

He was returning to the village through the hills when he came upon a group of people gathered around something on the road. My hand touched his face. They seemed to be in a knot around it, whatever it was, and Henry could not see. Peasants in their dark clothes, they made a dark spot, like a hole in the middle of the bright afternoon. They were muttering among themselves. Henry saw that they were immobile.

As he approached however, women began moving away from the group and came toward him. Their appearance was fantastic. Covering their heads with dark green or black shawls, their faces were bone colored. Their eyes were deep set. They had been weeping. They were women of different ages but all assumed a likeness. One hand tightening the shawl beneath the chin, they were almost gliding toward him, the other outstretched as if to touch Henry. The light managed to touch their cheeks just beneath the eyes, overexposing the skin and making it softly insubstantial. Their faces came closer, there were four or five of them now, and they placed their hands on Henry's elbows and shoulders. He could see now the dark hair parted in the middle showing just beneath the shawls. It was sometimes lined with grey above their eyes as black as any beetle if it weren't for the expression there, for the touch they had extended to him. Something was opening here. There were concentric circles of dirt around their eyes. Henry felt calm within their silence and was glad to be brought in. Their touch was at places skeletal and at others tender. He looked in their faces to find this same variety, but every face had become similar with grief. Their dark clothes were like a blanket. He was being brought in. To someone looking from the air it would appear as if an amoeba of peasants had swallowed him. Henry smiled at this.

At this moment he chanced to look up. Had he not, perhaps he would have missed it. For there, above the peasant's heads, hung an angel with its wings outspread. The people gathered must not have seen it since none of them looked up, though its feet seemed at times as if they were about to touch the crowded faces. At first Henry was unable to take his eyes from the massive wings. The blue shadows that hid in their undersides transformed themselves from complicated meander to images resembling hills and countryside, as in a Chinese painting; and then faces, lightly implied, became others. It was as if coming this close to earth, the undersides of the wings had become mirrors of it. But the blue shadows never completely substantiated any image. There were vines growing in the massive wings. The broad leaves imitated the plumage where they nestled and were turned silver by the dust. The wings themselves spread out from the angel's body like two great impossibilities, more militant than any explosion. Slightly asymmetric, touched by actuality, they shadowed Henry beneath them. He began to look at the angel itself. Its feet and legs were as still as stone. When it happened to come closer to the peasants' heads, its hands were transformed to talons. It then beat its wings again to keep itself at a distance. It looked up, not below at them. Its face was glory. Balancing light upon it, the flesh of the angel's face was separate from the light. The light around it brambled a nest for it out of the air. The tops of the angel's wings were turned pale by this nest. There, making itself commonplace above the voices, the angel remained. Praise slipped between its fingers and fell like the distributaries of some great river upon the heads of the peasants.

Henry could see why they had gathered beneath it. He was now near the center of the little crowd. There, on the ground at its center, was an overturned cart. Under its weight lay a young man who had been pinned while trying to repair a wheel. They had cleared the fallen hay off of the young man's face and body and it remained strewn about him on the road. Its smell lingered with that of the peasants' bodies. Women's voices reminded the helpless men not to lift the cart until the doctor arrived. The ox, still in its harness, lay on its side pawing at the air. Young children tired of waiting kicked dust into its mouth and eyes and laughed and ran each time it shuddered. Henry asked a middle-aged man who was lighting a cigarette, "Is there nothing to be done?" The youth's hair was a reddish brown beneath the dust. He bore a resemblance to the child Solomon who had carried Henry's bags to the hotel. But this one was years older. Two old men became hysterical. One slapped the other who only glared back in silence. There was something to this idea of burial. The cart itself was not merely a weight but had splintered on one side in its fall. A woman came forward with a blanket but then not knowing what to do only folded it over her arm. One no longer suffered the sensation of heat, the last of midday was gone. A dark haired man with a clown face began yelling at his wife, "I don't care what you say, I and my friends here will take care of it." He nodded at the men standing with their sleeves rolled up beside the cart and was dismissed with laughter. The sun had a drunk's face. The doctor arrived. The youth was weeping beneath the cart. The man with the cigarette looked at Henry and shrugged.

Henry had a child. Not much to be said here, the little bird not being particularly bright or beautiful or even plain. He gave her my name but I'm afraid she has lost the majority of her substance since his death, now only a small voice muffled by the telephone receiver or the panicked childwail one had to keep swatting away beside the open grave. She is now more a bee than a bird. Henry holds what he has of her somewhere as sediment and water in a dish beneath a potted plant. He does not move it or reach for it, but it is there nonetheless. She untangles her own little knot away from him, without him. Henry in the silence of hell gives no thought to a broken strand.

Like some form of clay, this silence. Henry, Henry watches two women standing by the dry fountain in the center of the little square. Notebook Henry notes that they are talking to one another but that the sound of it is not reaching him. That one is young and one is middle-aged. That they have placed their dark colorless baskets on the rim of the fountain and that their arms rest on them in almost identical ways. That he has made their faces gentle whether they are or not and that the distance between him and them is insurmountable. But most of all he notices that the silence seems to be gathering about them. They are pulling it in. The silence has been removed from where Henry sits and nothing has been left in its place. Two women in the center of the plaza are making a jug of silence that slowly covers their calves and arms and heads with the dim color of walls.

Henry took his dinner with some of the villagers in the bar at the bottom of the hotel. The talk was mostly politics—an upcoming election. Henry found himself talking about things he hadn't thought in years, at one point even scolding no more than a boy for speaking without experience. Someone laughed at something Henry said, and the man with the cigarette, the one Henry had been standing next to earlier that day, shook his head, "Yes, yes. Very clever. But what I would like to know is how long you will be staying with us." He turned out to be a petty bureaucrat, apparently the village was large enough, who walked tourists around, when they were there to be walked, for what little money could be made.

"We'll see," Henry said.

"It's not all blossoms," said the boy Henry had scolded, proud of having thought to say it. The men ignored him and went on talking about the election, would it be this one or that one?

Someone came in with news about the kid who had been trapped beneath the cart. He was fine, a couple of broken ribs at worst. The doctor had already left the house to attend to more serious matters. Which turned out to be the clown-faced man, who had shot himself with a pistol in the chest shortly after returning home. Even as the doctor arrived, the clown-faced man whose name was Cesare, as Henry now found out, had to be held down by his brothers as he heaped curses on his wife who had become hysterical in the next room. There had been a lot of blood and he wasn't expected to survive the night.

"To Cesare," said the man with the cigarette, and some of the others smiled.

The one who had come in now slapped himself in the forehead like an actor in a stage comedy. How could he have forgotten? The others didn't know. The real news was that the neighboring village had caught fire.

Henry stands at the window and the night sky is turned red by Cesare's blood. The bottoms of the clouds that stretch across everything glow with the life inside bellies or coals. Shadows have crept into the crevices of the red pillar of light. The distance—the very meaning of this word is destroyed by the risen blood in the clouds. Fire has not only been carried to him but has engulfed him with its shapes. There is a wound that has simplified the hole of the sky. The smoke and clouds chalk an imagination of fire. Henry remains untouched.

He escapes the redundancy of morning because he is ill. Through the afternoon he remains in bed and the stomach cramps steadily worsen. He has become feverish but not much; he asked the maid to call the doctor. If the stomach cramps continue, he knows that by evening he will be screaming. The maid enters and tells him the doctor will soon be here. Henry is in hell, he is sure this will be a relatively simple matter. A long dull day. The doctor arrives as its punctuation begins to be unbearable. He mumbles something under his breath about foreigners. Henry is not sure whether he is meant by this. After barely a look the doctor tells him that perhaps he shouldn't make such a fuss over indigestion. Henry refrains from calling him a quack. The doctor goes on to rebuke him for wasting his time and to say he is sorry no one told him Henry is a hypochondriac. Henry is furious; but the pain emerges from its hole and weakens him. He hears someone singing outside his window beside an old tree.

Those were difficult times. Henry remained in the village on the outskirts of hell. It was a period when he wandered without direction, as if he had pennies to give to children. As if he were a young man about to name his dream and not the old man he felt himself to be. He stood in the shadow of the trees. The time has come to stop continuing Henry, to end this note. Hell was not ready for him yet. He spent his days spending them, a bird pecking at crumbs in a silent plaza, waiting to arrive.

Globo

The children fell like water. They gathered about the light, stupid things against the small fire. The wind passed into my coat and I could smell the trees. The wind was a bad sign. I laughed at their bobbing despair covered by the pointed shields of the leaves. I wanted only the night here, though the dark was the conceit of a master about a closed flower, something to be crushed. What wild notions the hills have.

Palms to it, managing to be gentle for once—it wouldn't hurt to start looking for a place to sleep. There was nothing to remember, believe me. And yet they are beautiful like that, their faces radiant. I had once found night by looking through a needle of light too, not so extraordinary here after all. But the possibilities, it's throwing words into the daily mud just to think about it.

I have nothing here. As if in the old room, its velvet confessing to me, the darkness has shredded its curtains for bandages over a wound. Some emergency gilt with shore birds, invisible here, gone. I ran when I felt their massive shapes pressing down upon me. It was nothing, the daydream of a child on the stone steps of a church. But not now here hidden, not a dream here in the hills. The hiding has turned black with fear. Please don't tell me over a half broken phone that the leaf has exploded, that its map is now illegible to me.

These children. What can I ask of them, their hair cut like epaulets by their mothers. To let me open this pillow case I've taken to carrying, with the stain of my sister's spit still on it. To dump out its contents and show them what. That houses are burning in ways they shouldn't burn. That the flames have become responsible.

No, I'll blind the old Maquinista first, and take his few coins and let them sing in my pocket. The light is reflected off them a little ways on the plain. They jump to lift it, but jumping won't do it.

115

The salt and water and bone rolled toward me. They won't manage it, with all their talking. Another excuse to lift their arms. The sky was open before my fear was jagged enough to loom over them, to shadow them in a darkness woven with small needles, with minutes. Their fingers are a crest, a bit of air beneath a carpet. Seeping between their bodies, the dust seems lit with movement, but it is the imperturbable sand between the fingers of the long hand of water. The sky was a village. At its foot, every day might have left, by taking the small boat that was abandoned there. By pulling on the oars with the faith of fear, out past itself, past its own sewage. By imitating the bird that flew with its belly just above the drowned, seeming to graze upon the air.

Experience will only buy my death. They don't know they hold it. A bird's cry, found dead the next morning, that's the way to lift. The light detaches itself from the children's hands. With small shivers. The wind hides my sounds up here on the shoulders of the old men huddled together for miles. It shovels shadows over my face and I continue to live. Who am I? Where am I going? I tell you with all goodwill that these things are none of your business. And yet you continue to bathe my head as if I were a child.

The light has banished the wind from the plain. The wind hides with me in the clothes of the old men. This red shirt, what a stupid detail to have forgotten. Night has always been illegal. How many trees can I name. Seeing. They have come back! My friends have come back marching together, some wearing death, a little chalkboard on a string around their necks. And the words I have said over the distance between us fall asleep and dream.

It rises, this paid for light. Over the flowers in the gardens rooted in years. Away from the children's hands that like ruffled feathers have felt a first parting. I tell the wind again to shut its mouth, enough of questions you can't have. Away from the ground slowly, the light shows off its skeleton of days as if it were a gold tooth, as if it were a bowl of hot milk in the center of a storm. The children run beneath it.

The children are irredeemable, laughing. Their noise passes through broken ears. In a braiding of brutality, they hit one another in running streams of tears. A red reproach of blood from a nose, as each one is the one who was hit, blind. And such a thing to have nested, it holds them in sight for a moment. The spark of the rising world in their live eyes. Children, you have set loose a danger on the air, a spear hurled into the blackness. Do not listen beyond the spell of your years like a handful of stones. Remember the soaring bird you saw over the water.

I didn't remember the days, each marching with a rifle over his shoulder. It floats from them like a childhood nickname above jeers and paths and milk. I stood and looked at it. Innocence wears an old mask and eats the dust. The time has come to refuse his money. Looking back was like the flash of a fish showing itself. Farol. Be careful, boy, when you pick up that stick. You are just a sack of blood. I wouldn't have seen a thing if it were not for the leaves hiding me.

I hadn't moved for days. There among the little flowers, I gathered my days. Still it was time to move and yet the wings fell away from me. I had answered what I could hidden, and now simply collapsed. Sun in the day followed by unpredictable nights. I lay there fallen. The dark slowly began to gather around me. The lucky silence was a bad sign. They scream, their moon faces idiotic beneath the contraption. The land puts its shoulder against a great water that is coming on. The instinct to move had run out. I fired the last of my luck at them. The dead wind dreams the smell of sulfur for a moment and yet forgets it. I hear something falling with the weight of a body down the face of the hill. Were there birds in the air above me. The work I had done meant so little. Clouds came like mansions and erased it. Time is here in my coat, measured out. In small morsels. I have mixed together what comes to me over the night, and now in the folds of my shirt I find crumbs. The light illuminates a thousand losses. I didn't move.

High clouds came in on the still air and the light separated itself from the children. Silent as it gently rose from them, it looked like a paper lantern held by an unseen hand over their faces. But the dark was handless, and the light moved with wandering attention into the gaping doorway of the sky. Still at the threshold, it was graceful in its drifting. The children have lifted it. I see it there above them in the dark. There was nothing between them and it. They were free from each other. There was something between them and it. Soundlessly, the distance removes the last of its geometric conceit. The children see it. I had eaten all that I had brought with me. They and I watched it as something too far away now, as something forgotten. We watch it, as imperceptibly, and yet with perception only, the blackness erased it. Fusilado. The leaves fell onto the ground like empty shells.

The Lathe

Everything turns to shit. Assume an absolute turning. As if the stars were assholes. A quiet charm to it all. A quiet chasm unburdening itself of all of this. The sophistication of the world's turning, humbling. Perhaps if as you see some work accomplished I were to devoutly mold a little this for that. Impossible. Forgotten mid stream lost like a tune to a toothless whistler. As if perhaps one chair. Well. Then. Well made sturdy and not craft heavy. Simple, yes that's best. Then—as you can see, quite impossible. Then I might begin. As it is—well you can see for yourself. Moving in a circle with beginning outside of it. I huddle and this and that. Noodling about. Is it time? Ha, the groper watches the clock. Cursing. In my little shack. I favor most of the daylight with my trembling. Keeping busy here and there, occasionally losing a sweater button in the process. How accomplished. Wearing my delusions like a felt hat. This is the danger, you see, this getting in the swing of things. The blade will catch and I may lose another joint or two. Good god. The last time—blood upon the wall—the harpies rising from the town beloved and the hospital people tired. Keeps me awake, a little clip now and then without the roses or the cost. Been losing parts of my body this way for some time. Will have turned myself completely into wood soon. Keeps track of things. Is it time then? As I was going on—that there cost me my left thumb. This here, this charming little this, cost me a goodly piece of wrist. There we are, so much the better. So difficult to find a good hiding place anymore. As I was saying about the harpies. Hard on himself. Would almost be amusing if it didn't go on so. On so. Charm is a rare thing at any length. Perhaps I babble as I work. In the tradition. Well it must be time by now. And it is. Lunch. Here we have it—a flat white plate with two hard-boiled eggs, a slice of ham for that kick I so admire. Two large cups of coffee and I'm off again. Everyday. Gives me the lie of rigor. Thin at best, all this

119

inhaling and exhaling and chest thumping. Returning to the shop, the good old shop, invigorated and enthused. No, no, the charm is stifling. Back in my harness, I give it the go with a little here and perhaps a slap there. No harm, since concentration and decision elude me like two fat little twins with dirty faces. Perhaps whisperings. Perhaps a nervous condition. Ha, nothing so prestigious. The sniveler thinks he hears the murmurs of eternity. I am quite pedestrian. I finish things everyday. Composing the maze, watching the child hit the face of the water, I am indifferent to all that now. Just my meager grumblings left to plane and sand and finish. Done. Completely useless. In the end it will all be kindling, finished as you like. Failure and applause. Pirouette and shudder. A bit of payment? The bald pebble lifts and we see the two expectant eyes? Beginning is a sly joke. The talk that has taken its place destroys itself. Waste carved from waste and huddle. Is this the polite sound or the rude sound? It is useless and ornaments itself. The visitors whistling in the trees outside my little shack. It seems the world is full of chatter.

Then died. Thrown over the fence, undone. Spoken. A wreath of spoken over, uncrying.

The spinning makes it simple. As it was, a room. Remaining turning yet diminished, on time's lathe. Its thread the white and black part of silver under the wood chipped spinning threading through the blur and shedding slipping out tunnel and worm. A wire liquid salved by cotton and adhesive tape wrapped about its branch bone. Pass, sound through a trumpet bellow handed willow switch like wealth in bright coins that spin and sit. Under the swirl and out through the current's lips where birds have dipped their chests. A piece of metal has peeled the swarm from off the spindle as it streams and scatters the empty metal cans and bends the light around a pole, leaving it there. Thin through the center, the very spine of all this wishing. Held there in a long thin box, like a pool cue, hands and pressing where dangling haggard the figure is a marionette seeing and turning. When remembered willows reminded me of the silence and I fell out from under it and began to lose that day. Small feeling of balance, small incidental spell of sight and voice. Rhythming and tumble to recover a foreign composure. A man is seen in a dark green suit walking where the grass is well mown and he need only pass from the shadow into the light and admire. See how the breeze respects his bushy hair. The white hair leaves a shadow upon the face. Fittings bent down from the wall found where web and mud had grown slime the touched and guessed brown wet. The silence of slow moving insects in flowing gowns and black and white of the formal world. The fingertips of grief wove a web upon the ceiling of the room. What is left behind in the child's hand, in the afternoon chair or the high scream pronouncing loss down like a spire. In the morning where the sour light has touched the bed and touched as I here this and then there, out straight past the last twitch lost and heavy beneath the furrow. Past, past, past the last burden's acheheavy sigh and the look of objects when alone. Sad movements rustling in open places where people have gathered alone yet again. Gathering up, their expectations like broken birds whose legs have withered in the ash and mumbled. Past wind and fire and her face. Hung out to stop. Stop the silent intimacy in the yellow light. Stop the muscle and siren in the bird's throat. Stop the child's laughter and the child's fear as he stands by the bed touched with pale light. More stop than even the chipped white cup in the shadow-livened place.

There is a story that has passed through time with the strength of a swan's neck. It is about a man who was dying. A foreigner in a village of whispers. It is not this story, nor of this story, but illuminates these words like a distant porch light. The man was lying upon a bed in a strange village in which the rain puddled orange where it mixed with the clay. He lay in a dark moist room. The voice presses on these words to return to this place here,

the story of these words, but for a little while the eyes of
the speaking must rest elsewhere to find their way back.
There is only one way. The foreigner felt the cracks of the
walls in his lungs. There was a sun hiding out away
somewhere in a vigorous silence and immobility. In the
room there was only his wet breathing. The words trace
a path. The only passage is not a bridge but a well worn
wandering. To die lost among strangers, this is what the
man thought. Each day he waited to leave the small
village. Where would they carry him? His eyes closed
slowly and reopened. His shoes had been lost somewhere
and he had forgotten what they looked like. He stared at
his bare feet. In the afternoon he waited for a breeze
whose tone was unspeakable. He felt it in his dark hair
and in the creases of his crude hands. Just behind it, as
if the breeze had brought him, everyday there came a
thin large eyed child. The foreigner turned his head to
watch the serious child come in from the light. *Hello,
small bird*, the foreigner said in the child's language.
This was one of the two things he said. The small child
kept his face and arms very clean. His hair was combed
as well, though his legs and short pants were spattered
the color of the clay. The foreigner moistened his lips to
listen. The child sat on the ground beside the bed. He
came to tell the dying man riddles. He told them for about
two hours each day. Mostly short, and in his language, as
if he were reciting. If they had answers the child did not
speak them. They were like a slow music to the foreigner.
Though he did not know why the child came to him, each
day when the child was finished he smiled and said in the
language that was strange to him, *it has always been this
way*.

First and second line, the slow passing not passing
lingering in the dead world between the first question
and the first sadness in answer. Finding in the air an
area to occupy, unfurling its fabric, sounding the white
billow of aspiration out to pass in. Dissipate out, silence
finding its paths. The weed choked driveway denies with
its contours as the slow trudge, as the sun scrapes against

the gravel ruts beside the house. Miracle and fever lost along the steady path to the cottage. Within, the shadows are weathered and hot. The ceiling has separated and the walls are falling out where only the absence of the window remains all window all passing fabric up against the not face not hands not wonder. Further merely a concoction of the weather, without veil, without inside. To be unsounded, in the slipping gear's interior. The hour itself is remote, not just from what we have asked of it, our collage of kissing motion, or from our words that go tapping at its hollow, but from the figure it encases and branches forward. Where is the glue to paste the moment to the marionette. Hand found ticking, lips their whistle, the tall weeds hid their crackling and the color of the dirt where it touched their shafts and cut them and the old car approaching to thread what eye with solace. Along the brick wall there sat someone throwing stones out through the tall weeds, making hissing sounds as they cut their way and exhaling quickly before they stopped. Lifting again, out of silence the struggling heart of movement's color. The tilting pole within the heart. Bent forward and wishing for next and trumpeting the butchery of the moving figure as if her voice held the seed of a great pale cloud approaching silently with its blindness over the flat land. There is no triumph and the lost hands and legs are in every ditch in the world. But see the face threaded with its yearning, babbling incoherencies. The movement bent, the place where curling within the starting lay the dirge. Every touch of flesh leaves its color. Then the fall itself a farce. Un chien a pitycoats of play and sham. I was there and the eunuch bull, coagulation of being gathered was a pillar of the areas between clutching us and this. The clutching voice parting the willows with its shot. As in a circus, the spectacle is dependent on colored movements. Where the hat tipped laughter of the orange and green geometric catchings, something slipping away here, a well meant word disconnected there somehow and underlined in yellow. Amused at being caught and read passing over and away threaded

by a music staff the silent figure dances his dying. Then
still, like the weight in a sack. Like the rolling over of
every bulk. There is a festive coloring at the bed of the
path the voice takes. The rising color is uncovered like a
map that charts the path to the mountain's lip, to a web
of paths touched with colored turns as if the paths themselves were gathered up in the swirling breeze which has
disfigured and composed again the color as the edge of
something buried in the ground. Everywhere the voice
turns it finds a smudge of remembering catching on it
and muting its fury at moving toward silence. The glare
outside the house has become the white erasing all things
to leave the surface of what blind fabric. When they spoke
she asked why he was not speaking, and his answer had
the same look about the eyes it always had and there was
a touch here of listening, there of wishing to hand her his
words again. I hold what I can of you and wander out and
away as if I held together, as if I was one untrembling.
The passage where it says there was a green humming-
bird holding itself in the emptiness above a bright flower.
Caught, unsaid in the unweaving of our past gestures.
The loom held vestiges of a thrown bottle shattering, lost
occurences as it lost pieces of yellow thread that had
described a small comic figure whose limbs would not
move except to dissipate and whose voice, as though
trapped in the tension of the loom, could not find its way
from thread to air. She turned and looked out the window. The objects that could be seen through it slowly
slipped in to and out of shape. At times it seemed as if
there was a light behind them, at others the light seemed
to be in them. They had a storybook quality about them
and the quiet made it appear as if they were made of clay.
They touched only to continue the farce of seamlessness.
The lines bent slightly but only to let the rug and floor
receive the light that now was coy now was gentle. The
voice has fallen and lies upon its battered wings in the
street, it murmurs. Gather all the flashing myth and
worry out its verifying sense from where you have found
it in the bulging shapes of dying animals along the

roadside weeks ago, in the sound of a catastrophic snapping passing to you over the noon air, in the vision of an old man falling from a ladder. Every vessel of continuing broken, yielding up something dark and redder than blood, continuing. Feel the texture of it, small yet heavy in the ground. Draw the reel and fin the plow hand in the disc of the sun's afternoon like a clock hand in its light on the never broken land scratched and waiting for the shadows and the slop. A fat man walked along like a cripple, slip linger, heaving his torso forward, small scuffle, hoping the rest will follow. His face was a pouch for he weeps. His head is a white block bleeding the red face. He finds the smooth wall of the world and breaks his block of crumbling against it. There is nothing left of him, not even the shame in the paper silence.

To balance a wheel, to hammer it flat and pass the surface of order along its rim. The axle hidden in the thicket of spokes is the knuckling disturbance. Shudder forward under the wingbeats of the moment's mechanism. In the dark noise to find a nest of worry and cherishing. A large clay bowl filled with still water. Plunging your head into the cool center of the wheel, feel the divots of its rippling as you lift your face. The cold air separates itself from the wilting figure. Alone, the figure suffers from order. It is forever distinguished, attempting entanglements like a parody of sympathy. Now you have seen a luminous mechanism, a weight of light in a dark place, now you see your hands assembling it from cold nails and fibers. The lines of thread extend into the rocks that have the substance of sounds. The webbed nest of a water bird as fallen as the pecked sounds and the bar of cloud that has made the sea a shelf and the breeze a hesitancy is the clay sun that hangs behind it, still. This is what you have asked the light lying on objects, holding them still as eggs upon the kitchen table, its dialogue with you your tether to the day and spinning of things. The will of silence is quick around the reckoning voice as the last words deny anything but the leaves lifting from the ground like a vertical tunnel, like a shape of swirling. Where has the light found refuge. There in the air's fabric, its sinews converging. Silence and again the yearning breeze. The trees leave refuge in softly shaped blankets beneath. But all that towered was a menace to grief, extending its hands along the ground and leaning above touch. There is no hammer stroke or bell insinuating moments. Only a small stepping sound cherished in the gravel there, a figure fallen in a nest of wire. The wide fall bent its head and knew the dark expanses brown on the bent hillside. The tall chap carried over his into the fall's ring over and again the stones carried over them along the hill's rim and still the tightening ran through his neck through his hands. He unsang the mumbling over the hole cut by the box-fire and continued via cloth via absolute words bent like metal rods entwined into the shape of her hand on a wheel. There is no end to the tendernesses and no beginning no finding and no touch that has not become sinew and howling. Press out the last fire lingering in the glance. Through the center of the wreath and the chewing gum wrapper, there is no whale or furnace to encase you now. A chance meeting with movement, kissing the lipless jug of time from without. Dropping over the hedge again feeling earth before bearings or roses distinguish themselves from the self-same vessel. Did ground catch or out away passing thud on nonsense and the season like a flowing thing, its passing point through the gate worn open and down, red chipped visible. The grass bent around the hospital's white bulk behind the trees' tender faces, and passing blank swept out toward you hollering her yellow passage, you grieved. Unhappened how hands have risen, palm up sang toward afternoon with its haze and rumble weight beburdened down from shoulder, heart, needle. Thrush, she said, and the bundled shadow passed over the contour of the sheet where the window light touches it and her fingers rested lightly on the open page of the small clean book. A silver object in a lost room, the socket where the absolute brutalities have smoothed out the hard surface. The very light itself submits to possibility, humbled by the fever of an arcing line, drawn to call itself some shape. The forms haunt every birth and leaf, whispering symmetry and strength. And the tangled flesh that ornaments the bone is as shapeless as the breeze. See it hang and, red and ungainly, oppose itself. Falling, its bulk is again newly proportioned. A piece of something cut that stinks with time. With time all the lunging shapes are slaughtered and the red streaked ribs hanging can no longer hide even the murmur of a clinging wish. The palest bed held the palest light. Hand passing out to what open song, into it. Over the sad laughing into all the hanging prayers and past her where seeds cling to the hem of her skirt and passing her, diminished and unhinged yet still afire and moving, still hitting the objects and fashioning them from wind and absence, still holding their spark for a moment, still remaking them in the image of loss hounding the shadows of a dark place, filling them with brass and oil, filling them completely. Passing her, her voice shook loose the light and let it wander. Away it shattered, in an instant the distinct web was and was gone. A woman walks. The world has shook something in her loose from it and yet. The soles of her feet where they touch the deep sound are the only coherence, the only continuing hum.

There was a terrible fire. Look, there is no reason for this voices in the dark business, since the ship gave its innards to the birds. It lay there on the sand, broken at its middle. Its concrete bulk sent forth rusted steel rods into the air, bobbing from the wind and children's hands at the waterline. There is an inside to it, where its back was broken. A down in there, the salt cold crawling in the dark. There are children's faces in the sunlit holes. Crabs pass over the shattered floors. The colors seen through the holes are incredible greens. The ship lies disemboweled on the sand. Children pass over it like crabs, and the water comes to eat it away. It has come upon its resting place with a great grinding and now is being washed to nothing. On dark days, the person strolling in the evening will find it attempting to distinguish sea from sky. It will seem like a massive grey foundation with shoots of metal sprouting from it. It will seem wide and fallen. More than ever it will imply a ruin. Sand around it is smooth and wet. On this close hot day the sky seems to be blurred, or a series of stains. Birds hover over the water's hushing sound. The place is deserted. There is a cliff with a row of trees along its rim behind you. Steps cut out of the cliff. A clear sound of falling has found you on this beach. It hovers around your head, washing it. You pass over the contours of the ship and feel the extent to which you have been crippled. Perhaps the fall, perhaps something else. You lie resting, your face pressed to a slab of metal that is cool now that there is no sun. Should you wait for the dome of stars and the moment of wonder? You decide against it and begin to move again. You find one of the holes the children stick their heads through. You begin to lower yourself down into it, down until you drop and land on something in the dark. Here you will lie suspended forever. Here you may disintegrate in peace.

Things continue moving. Straight ahead and then on, flat ahead plain and single. A slight movement and then level. Back on. The point a lie unwound to rhythm undone. There is voiceless to fill, lessening out of absence. Black opens back against stop. Hesitancy left in the dirt to crumble and uncrumble again. Hands have wished extension from a tube, and hang like wasps in the minute. The wormless sifting, losing duration with passage. On less through. The word left touched, crowing a still thistle. Figure in the doorway, glare touched face glare touched hands, shadow cradled hair silence washing her palms. First beheld then lost. Stitched into remembering, stuttering. Death is always a three o'clock breeze, passing through anonymous branches along a well kept walkway, with clean handrails where the cement has been neatly portioned off in rectangles. Summer slips away from the other seasons, flat as a word to be pasted, looking for a hovel in which to carve its sun alone. The rain has sent its sliver to the bone. Folded neatly along a sharp edge, curling in a burnt leaf. The tilting rod has found its equilibrium. The sound stops. Once or less upon a hard nest where the greying grass. So uh so we so so then so. The dim weight of sand stone in the figure walking, the outline in hammered leaf in the afternoon. The figure up to the waist in round stones, exhaling sympathy and the contours of roots showing at the base of muddy trees. Dried and split, the figure cracking its apologies to the mist. Tangled in a thicket, silently caught in passage by high vines. The air and the sea are filled with promises of stopped motion, and yet the only snare is sound. See the chicken blood on the fencepost and the last of the paint on the shed. Every marking is the sleeve of movement, but there is no arrival and no song. The figure is held by the spear of geology, and all the strangers who searched over the flat heavy place are dead. They have fallen upon each other like a box of nails spilt out on a cement floor. A house held by stars and the comic figure whose baggy pants were the mountain line, whose face was the mesh of twilight. The moon pressed to place sheds yellow crayon. The voice had fashioned itself into its movement from a strip of tape, cotton, and wire. It wished and fell and turned beneath the humped tones. Measure and buckle sunder me down to the grain's scratch and up to what a whistle holds in its shell. Where do the dead sleep when it gets cold, and where the living. When the cold is no longer a stone but the breath between the bitter lying down and the bone. The brick benches are still beneath the dark trees. Shades in the breeze along the ground drawn up like tents, inhaled by the masses of leaves. A meander half in shadow, tracing off upon a stone wall. All its strands entwined in an unknown direction. Reaching back, lost forward. Yet followed forward, each sinew rises recovered separate before plunging again within the fabric. The fingers of the pattern catch the light as it pulls away its taut wires. The hull is full of fire, the planks crack exposing their meat. One tilt and teetering all stopped poised shoulder-heavy. Then the chinese cloth has caught flame and the falling sailor's head breaks like a chestnut. The roar and turn and again the stopping when the converging moments become again as faceless as the sea. As still as the sloping hillside and the mist comes down, still higher than a child. The dark of things beneath it distant where green has turned to shale. The wet air in the gorge resolved in silence and a brown leaf. There is nothing beyond the bark of the trees. The paths fall. That without grace stumbled. That without touch spoke. Under the wishing weight sang his trident bellowing words without and within, where his laughter shook the mud from the cracks of his sad shack. Without the wherewithal to diminish, fell and being whittling away the figure, whittling away the mist, away the cantata of faces and the empty fist beneath the sheet beneath the silent procession of births. Of was and hands have found this dreary breeze among mornings like dark birds. This breeze has found man's stumble and clutch and humiliated it as if it were a song. The pines were anemones of shadow in the evenings. To diminish oneself in favor of grace. This and sputter falling a toy plane, red and magnificent tensions drawing its lines. Clouds held what was left of the light along the curved sky. Not to recall his name further except as silence further into the mechanism of room and open air and the calling voice except as a child of his inattention walking out into a crowd. The sounds of birds attached the trees to one another with night. Sleeping beneath blankets and grasping while a piece of pale green ribbon was caught on the ground by the hospital's light. To diminish the object of one less and less remembered, of pale rhythm.

We see. Something constructed up left, held. Worn shape from holding. See there left staying past. The shape of the stone rising from the wet ground more than outline more than bulk. Hewn out of air. This continues to be done where the bleached green hood of the abandoned truck hunches beneath the tall grass. The trash is denied by the ground. We see. All the lost meat and the gained breath. The shaped hedge curving and the light leaf are cracked and swept again by a flat sky without a face that will only speak the gurgling of planes. What place has weight here where the bell tones follow the streets to the house. White and texture wrestle for every shape as it falls down into the whirring silence of the earth. Every stumbling is a disc in the spine of the figure lying long beneath the green range. A series of things almost discerned through the brush, in the trees. Becoming almost complete before unraveling with distance and then the next perhaps merely a continuation, looming and elusive. The figure is one direct downward stroke in the light. The empty trees and the clay beneath. As if to construct a tree, as if to hinge each branch. The empty trunk like a cylinder for the figure, where it might develop its face from chicken wire bent to contact and wear. See the stone contours of the eyes. The graph within the leaf is siphoned through the face and hands. The figure is a downward stroke to the ground. The vertical reaches for its thwarting.

Not a blue cavern or forged from blue but in an empty blue vastness. The blue umbrella is the illusion of coherence, of the parallel. Bright without conscience or splashing. Perhaps its own carnival music, the falling blue spray beyond from. Its chemical without would smell like bleach if it were not empty. Place the drawn x anywhere and hope to have begun. Light passing through it entirely alone. Wishing speaks of a shimmering sheet but is without hands and falling. Wishing imagines an under of islands and flat stones. Of simple sticks, of the light finding an object. Down—the fall like knees and necks on the steps until the hounds come sniffing. Snapped. The great machinery is clacking, ever fond of its grinding down. Horned and braiding unleashed feathers in the air. If there were bells and tourniquets to service this clamor. Hammered clicking, giving small resistance and then forward, like a bicycle. The engine in your chest down the steps. The arrowhead of your face chips at brief touch. The ground is a lover. The dull

ground-hitting ferris lights in the cranial bucket. The
small mangled flower of you left. The dust rising, your
corona. Continuing down undone in blue continuing.
Your back arced, your broken fingers splayed, anticipating. I? Why I lost the last of my face and hands beneath
buried in some round hum in the nut of the world.
Something in which to have lost and imagine foundation.
Beneath and washed. Beneath its pearled ridges, the
water is fibrous and dark. Here and there in the silence
many voices huddle in a fossil against the cold pressing.
The bones of water make skeleton huts. From the still
ribs I turn pale faces toward my resting place before I
begin to rise. The shudder of movement is cool. I feel it
rising in long fibers to the shallows. I break off in all
directions, hump out to many deaths in the single ringing. The world is deep with dark and the bone's touch. I
fragment down beneath, where I have found a drum. My
children's wings are white and silent as they tear me
open in the air. The light has talons to lift. I bend my
head to the rising. The rocks along the waterline are
pecked to pieces by the wind. The creases in my hands
channel the blood off my arms and through my fingers.
My face is eyeless and dark as I am lifted into the
shallows of the clouds by all the children lifting me
skeletal and fashioning trumpets from their laughter
clamoring above the world. Or the churchlight in the
trees, sifting myself there of green and dark. Over the red
fox and the sour taste of grass, without looming, with
slow movement over the quivering passages, thickening
every pocket with just the sight of seeping in. In among
the afternoon and morning being merely a matter of
angle. Shards upon the living ground. At the altitude of
respiration and entanglements. Scrambling without tra-
jectory and ever sifting her eyes where they have been
the shadows of an owl passing to collect. And something
in fabric makes it precious beneath the trees. Across and
over sifting the minutes for the dust slipping from the
needles in the light that has unstuck itself. In the woods
where I had seen a poor woman sleep without fear or

awareness of glory upon the roots of a giant. Filling my lungs with the soft sound of her fatigue and hiding from her in a burrow with a small frantic darkness. Intersecting bodies have amassed each other and the green tiers, green wings which beat slowly where the huddle of living is a knot ambling toward extension. Moving over the curved world cocooned by mist, only to be snatched up, snared and lifted by arm or foot or neck. Up again up this movement stopped hung up, dangling from the heart of wires over a city. Bobbing in a compromise and again denied and comic. Flailing at tick, lunging toward upside when tick and the slickness of the wire rising from your midsection toward what. The city of animals and glass your hands and feet take turns brushing. Its map of yearning and geometry. I see them there below moving about in concentric circles. Slabs of metal clanking in the lines. All easily diagramed moving. Remade and well dressed once, carrying small lights to one another, the miracle figures fill the blood vessels of the glass face. I sing them and attempt to tap a shoulder with my foot or hand. They bend forward continuing, hiding a canine or tusk beneath each lip. Everywhere they leave small round spectacles, everywhere they whisper beautiful connections and I can see the spots upon their hides. They make drums of the very pavement and string the lines they draw with hoofbeat words wanting to be thunder. I have wished myself bent strangely back over the lips of a woman I have seen and remembered. She speaks into my chest to people I no longer meet and feels my eyes beneath her fingers. Again I bend myself and my fancy trying to stay down or up but remain hanging in the blue without shape from a mobile above the world. The light touching your side and erasing the detail there. Up then down are two moments with their partition of flesh. This is the situation, the mobile turning in its faint music, this the context where you find yourself suspended. You hang, still in your clothes. It is mammoth. Where does it hang from. The heart of wires, where it extends its metal arms out, drops its fibers like a huge musical instrument.

At the end of a wire, your body approximating a spider, you pass over the birds and attempt to discern the faces of those others who must be hanging with you from the other arms in the buoyant air. You worry about the change falling from your pockets and about the difficulty of breathing in the simple suspension you have imagined.

If it could, if but then it could. A gentle face poised where Rosa saw its planes unfold, delineated and unhung until the eyes seemed to be those of a mandarin. The final beats where mystique has found a barren bird's foot. A chest of straw, if but a clown she might have known to pearl. Please and then return, Rosa as if speaking to a fountain, as if walking on the tiles of a mid afternoon she had seen that there bent around the corner what she had found to hold and became higher and wider than had been frightened from wishing without where the thunder laid a tapestry of her breath upon her patience and a brown basket hollering rosemary on the terrace. Had cracked Rosa became. Sang and came the gentle face. What brush, the pale house wore the sun on its pate and sad addition of passing. Apples. Rosa held the world in a face were it risen, where it had lain again sound beneath again and song before where on to where with hands and sullen reach always to touch and resume attempting to remove and touch again beneath no longer. Rosa, a victorian light in the halls. This is where the horrors of purity began again and the exact shapes crowd around his bed. Outside of breathing and its lurch, the geometric hung cold. A blue triangle, a red square, and a yellow sphere came to him like kings. The luminous and geometric, hovering in the air of his room. Found him screaming. Having made them he fell from them. Untouching made seen and imagined. Definition lit them like a pulse. They were pressing they had murdered him there was no touching them where they had become set forever where his room could no longer be imagined he said that. The several forms stepped out of the doorway of making, finished and brutal. There were no instances, where every line removed time. He asked them to dip him in his small fever where he might at least scream so they might find him but they would give nothing and he couldn't marshal the tensions in his throat or arms to name them because a triangle, a square, a sphere hung beyond and his voice could not rise at the arrival of order though he remembered its making. All the flesh and bed clothes fall away and the geometric is left, hovering and made clean, placing itself and waiting for place to corrupt it, yet unheld. The place we speak of here as if moving into it solidifies. The furniture as they speaking dancing hollering are furniture. Lost and have here details as if in a sack to speak of as if ordering making worthy and tidy her eyes green her words with that brittle aspect while he white oval in the window light hands fleshy denying bone and joint a small nightstand made of wood of brown smooth drawers where they pull out a blue car sounding scrollwork on the oval mirror a slight tip to the edge a rounded surface with a center say sphere hoping to grab something there three ribbons presumably dust here and the moving speaking hoping to said solid again sphere her eyes where they have been green the written name upon a scrap of paper pass into withhold I into undoing endowing the scrap of paper with a name having given that away freely like surface rubbing being thinned away the diameter of the cylinder having whittled away fear I thinning having come to floor scraps wrong combination of details wrong reassembling of what she had is wrong putting together again of had as if in a sack the green tossed away and unrecovered had her eyes ever had her eyes ever had they been her yes of course what were they of her face as she covered it with her hands had they meant her eyes had they meant tossed away from hands from thinning they shatter on the floor of everything her lost yes of course her lost next there losing back when movement had not meant loss of what being asked gathering together again from lost fragments on the ground no broken open without gathering never last thinning I bent back around the words her eyes continuing without cut slim and broken that room that sound falling wrong words wrong memory wrong I wrong combination thinning,

There is a sinew in the quiet dark, It is thin and reedy where it turns, has an idiot's face and open upturned palms where it has was and sounded reached within the figure cold beside the sleep wall and its trash, The hair like ruffled feathers where the bent neck pushed the hurt face down, The figure just before it is unstrung when the new sounds are not heard, The room is the same, It is dark and affords little and unspecified room, The shapes within it loom large and neither rest upon nor float above the floor, They are placed and are so distinct they cannot even huddle, They are severe and smooth, The luminous shapes have rope danced silently with the extreme. The grace of the hoop of walls is grey toward the edges. Listen there and hear it whistle its delirium. The definitions have a cadence that demands an altar of outline. A lathe and yet a lathe and so a sound that found its ringing in through threaded out the worry in my hands the lines whose features whelp around and a lathe spin the sound and pump of touch and rustle. And the weeping box that makes square angles of the grimaced face in crevices and shadows of a room beside the bed. Where from the window I have seen a figure seen in the distance like a distant figure only it was a stack of boxes she confided to me in the lathe of what we saw of each other where her arms rested on the sill and the lace quivered on the bed where the breeze had turned it into the touch of a distant figure. Leaving, threading some doorway, out we found our voices like manacled wrists in the grey of the street where there are two planes of buildings rising brown and grey almost with black windows and the milky shimmer of sun where the breeze sounds the trash and the overcoated figures have caught color and shaking its empty sleeves move along with their stoppages in their mouths and hands and bowels down that which has worn the soft hair off their heads. Mouth, hand, bowel, and the straw image in a bird's beak weave the ribbon weave the unthreaded song in the skull in the drum where only sitting sour and abandoned among the pigeons saw a spring across the park where the shadows had filtered gently between the light and the trees. Along the slanting edge out. Up beneath the darkened hover. It glowed back away around and out dark as if nuzzling inside these shadows. Soft red off of the closeted shapes like alcohol evaporating off the chest of a child but unsullied by associations. And a yellow sphere blunt colored and pale at its bulge. A large hanger and the mere side of a helmet, there like musical bellows and tubing. Geometric shapes glow all the refinery of pursuit in a dark room. The shroud with its rendered bluebells could not fill a thimble with its distinction of his features. The room's shadows retire the corners and the sound. But color from the geometric shapes has brought its detail like a thistle. In a quiet place, in an empty place. There the sum of holding something lost, in time. Turning in the sheet until the constriction became a comfort of home or a grey shadow upon the empty wall opposite. The pleiades hover over the head of the childless figure in its raincoat where she has paced the street and spoken the wind about her head. The few words held, the few words sounded. It was not that the bed had drifted. It stood solid and bowed where it always had, rumpled and possibly holding something more than rags, though little. It was that the bones were pipes beneath the grey flesh. The bones had elbowed and angled their way into something beyond them once again, from which they had come. And the bones were pipes and the pipes hummed. The humming was where the warmth of the afternoon had gone. And the bones that were pipes hummed and it was as if the humming drew the light. Drew it to the bed further than it had gone, regardless of season the figure in the street betrayed by light because its words were caught again by the wind and trash from the building's back upon its feet and ankles and conspiring with the building the light abandoned her. The moaning plumbing in the bed's final tangle knew nothing of the comedy of trash and wind and figure and only drew its own curtain of smell and ash. Two expirations, two figures held suspended in sound surrounded by silence, held there glowing and precise and planed smooth. The fanaticism of their harmony. The hand that left the shadow on the cave could not delineate the sorrow of a square, triangle, circle, square again and so on up along the line and bent around a wail beyond muscle and minute in the shadow of an unapproachable mechanism devising associations, k in the root of something simple, its physical example thin and hieroglyph, a gold letter c on a door in a hall. Step then step. Unbraiding this, becoming a solid untold presence or quality where moving along the lines of the forms like an ice skater. Trembling within the crepuscular trembling, in and of it. Coming to it, un un un, a wind up toy clicking and turning itself over as it runs out. I ask this of it, this I of it standing at the top of the stairs and then in mid air head beneath chest beneath feet, guessing at the hardness of the wood, I ask this threading through or at least at or at least its gesture must. To utter some resonant sound in the vessel before it is shattered. I to it, this relation's bridge. These words written while clicking. Say something, believe something as it shatters back through belief. No more words for where. Nothing but words for where. Speak, speak, stop. I of. I of gathering stuff of catastrophe patina humble humble coiled an airplane pilot gossamer unstuck floating down of the of floating summer bowed to touch ground spin return very and then of return up to then and and we found what might and might and might have been its course over and up to spool and return might run along clean easy lines except that all that made were what might be known of or without if such a thing might burn bulb is right since known of compulsory figures were crickets here where I that such a thing crickets, good continue if such a might as voice behind like a tailgunning solid stuff since collapse since packaging of continued no fire no box no wait and grasp have held have held did have made small cricket have was if could sun like a crushing roller yellow flattening had seeds if was could yes of run out was begin since unreturn run down could red, blue since outline was cricket cricket.